MW00682945

Angels Stars and Trees

Angels
Stars and Trees

Tales of Christmas Magic

by
John Forrest

Your Scrivener Press

Library and Archives Canada Cataloguing in Publication

Forrest, John, 1947-

    Angels stars and trees : tales of Christmas magic / by John Forrest.

ISBN 978-1-896350-25-7

    1. Christmas stories, Canadian (English). I. Title.

PS8611.O772A64 2007   C813'.6   C2007-904205-8

Book design: Laurence Steven
Cover design: Chris Evans
Interior and backcover illustrations: Tim Steven
Author photo: Courtney Whalen, *Orillia Packet and Times*

Published by *Your Scrivener Press*
465 Loach's Road,
Sudbury, Ontario, Canada, P3E 2R2
info@yourscrivenerpress.com
www.yourscrivenerpress.com

We acknowledge the Canada Council for the Arts and the Ontario Arts Council for their support of our publishing program.

Acknowledgements

The author would like to thank the places where his stories have appeared previously, in both print and broadcast format:

Belleville Intelligencer, Capper's, CBC Radio One ("First Person Singular," "Ontario Morning," "Richardson's Roundup"), *Chicken Soup For The Christmas Soul, The Front Porch, Good Old Days Christmas Special Anthology, Orillia Packet and Times, Orillia Today Metroland News, Pembroke Observer, Reminisce Christmas Book, Reminisce Extra, St. Catharine's Standard, Sudbury Star, Toronto Sun, The Tribune.*

To my beloved wife, my
"Christmas Carol,"
whose guidance, encouragement
and love have inspired and
supported me in all my
endeavours, and who truly is the
"magic" in my life.

Contents

Preface 9

Note to the Reader 10

Star of Hope 13

That Special Tree 37

The Gift of Time 49

The Elves' Christmas Tree 55

Oh Christmas Tree! 65

Last Minute Tree 83

Glass Angels 89

About the Author 119

Preface

Of all the traditions in the life of Canadian culture surely Christmas must be one of the most enduring. It reaches out each year to sprinkle its magic and wonder on all and sundry, while paying particular attention to the young; and even after those children have moved on in time, the magic of Christmas lives on in loving memory. And upon many occasions, it becomes so firmly fixed in the hearts of the young that its embers flare up annually throughout life, inviting the adult to enter again the wonderful warmth of the Christmas season.

John Forrest is one of those adults. Already equipped with imagination, energy and a generous warmth of spirit, he was ready, eager and willing when Christmas came knocking. As he grew to adulthood, his celebrated skills as a storytelling teacher and author gave him the tools to keep those memories alive.

Now they are offered to you, with the hope that they will awaken those that abide in your heart.

Read on!

Lloyd Dennis
O.C., O. Ont.

Note to the Reader

Dear Reader,

Thank you for choosing *Angels Stars and Trees: Tales of Christmas Magic.*

I began writing short stories to share recollections of the exceptional events and wonderful people who have touched my very full life. My happy childhood, those trying "teen" years, an exciting and interesting 35 year career in education and my role as husband and father provided me with a rich source of material. But in particular the celebration of Christmas holds a remarkable number of cherished memories and this anthology is the result.

All of these stories are based on actual events in my life and/or the experiences of people dear to me, but I must admit, in the fullness of time and retelling, to some embellishment. However, the basic facts and settings of the stories remain true.

Two stories, though, may require explanation. "The Gift of Time" is a childhood memory of my wife, my beloved "Christmas" Carol. It was written by me, as told by her to our children, 'neath the Christmas tree.' In "Glass Angels" the character Michael was a "city" friend with whom I played when visiting my aunt during holidays in Toronto. Although I have actually seen Mr.

Novak's tree and did spend time with Mike at Christmas that year, it was after the fact. The beauty and magic of the glass angels is revealed as seen through his eyes.

Also, the stories have been placed in this anthology for dramatic and literary effect. If you should wish to read them in chronological order, please begin with "That Special Tree" and follow with "The Elves' Christmas Tree," "The Gift of Time," "Glass Angels," "Star of Hope," "Oh Christmas Tree" and "Last Minute Tree."

May I add that the stories were written to be read aloud, as well as enjoyed privately. It is my sincere hope that their telling will prompt you to recall and share your cherished Christmas memories.

Enjoy the read and may the spirit and magic of this most special season forever touch the lives of you and yours.

Merry Christmas!

John Forrest

Star Of Hope

"Hold it right there!"

I froze in mid-step, pinned to the wall by a brilliant beam of light, blinded by its glare. The voice behind the flashlight echoed hollowly in the emptiness of the stairwell.

"Where do you think you're going?"

"Well, what now?" I thought. "How do I explain this one?"

The beam shifted a little lower, out of my eyes, and I was able to make out the shape of the uniformed guard who held the flashlight.

"Well, officer, you see, ah, it's . . . well, my wife is on the next floor and . . . "

Christmas Eve, 1969, and here I was, caught in the back stairwell of the Soldiers' Memorial Hospital, dressed in a Santa suit, toy bag over my shoulder, sneaking up to visit my wife Carol in the surgical ward. How could I make this stranger understand the importance of my mission? Carol and I were newlyweds and it was our first Christmas together. This, combined with the fact that Carol's name was a legacy of her December 25th birthday, made the celebration even more special!

The holiday season had begun well. We had thrown ourselves eagerly and completely into the spirit of things. Our tenth floor apartment bristled with decorations. Wreathes and tinsel abounded. Spray-on snow spattered the windows and mirrors, while seasonal towels and Santa soaps adorned the bathroom. And our tree was a thing of beauty. A shimmering cone of multicoloured light, it brushed the ceiling in the window corner of the living room. The Christmas cards had been mailed and our presents were already wrapped and under the tree. By Friday, December 23rd, our preparations were complete.

To begin the holiday weekend our friends from the seventh floor, the Hansens, spent the evening visiting and the eggnog flowed freely. We had a late night, and I had settled into a sound sleep when disaster struck.

"John, wake up!" said Carol, shaking my shoulder.

"Uh . . . what?" I mumbled.

"Wake up!" insisted Carol. "Something's wrong."

"What do you mean?"

"Well, I've been sick twice and my stomach is killing me."

"Too much eggnog?" I suggested.

"No, I don't think so." Her voice was tight with pain. "I'm really sick."

I reached over and snapped on the night table lamp. One glimpse of Carol's ashen complexion, pursed lips and the beads of sweat on her forehead signalled the seriousness of her condition. We headed for the hospital. The doctor in Emergency confirmed my worst fear. Acute appendicitis was the diagnosis. Immediate surgery was the treatment, and Christmas in the hospital was the prognosis.

Events moved quickly. After a brief conference with the doctor, we had a few mumbled reassurances and a kiss for luck; then they wheeled Carol off to surgery. Although she was suffering physical pain, it was clear from the look in her eyes, as she gazed up at me from the gurney, that this sudden disruption of Carol's Christmas plans would exact an even greater emotional toll.

At the nurse's suggestion I headed home to gather up the personal items Carol would need for her stay in the hospital, and returned just as she was being released from the recovery room. Shortly after 6:00 a.m. on December 24th Carol was wheeled into her room in the surgical ward. Though still groggy, she was alert enough to recognize my voice and squeeze my hand in response to my words of love and support. My stay, however, was brief.

The floor supervisor, Nurse Krause according to her nametag, arrived to greet the new patient and inspect the room. We exchanged greetings and then she added, "She needs her rest. Don't you think you should get some sleep too, Mr. Forrest?"

It was not a question. It was an order.

"Well, I'd like to . . ."

Krause's drill-sergeant voice cut me off. "Yes, I'm sure you would; however, she's my patient and she needs her sleep. Visitors are permitted from 1400 until 1900 hours. You can come back then."

There was no appeal. I patted Carol's hand, kissed her on the forehead, said my goodbyes and reluctantly took my leave.

I really was tired. The sun was rising but even though it promised to be a beautiful morning, I was ready for bed. I drove home, called Carol's mother from our apartment and broke the bad news. After the initial shock and a flurry of questions and answers, we cancelled the family Christmas dinner scheduled for our apartment, and planned a visit to the hospital instead. One more call to order flowers for delivery to Carol's room and then I fell into bed. I slept through the day and woke about 5:30 p.m. It was a different Christmas Eve than expected.

I showered and dressed, stopped for a burger on the way to the hospital and arrived in time for 7:00 p.m. visitations. Krause was off duty and her replacement at the nursing station questioned me only briefly before letting me pass. Carol was sitting up in bed, an I.V. line connected to her left arm, clad in the nightgown I had brought earlier. We exchanged greetings and I leaned over and kissed her. Her lips were dry and rough, but her eyes sparkled and despite the absence of makeup her colour was good. It was clear, however, from the tone of her voice, that her spirits were very low. Soldiers' Memorial Hospital may have been able to repair her body, but it was obvious that her heart was still broken.

Spending Christmas in the surgical ward would ruin all of her carefully laid plans.

Time dragged as we chatted. Small talk just didn't cut it and almost every comment I made seemed to remind Carol that she wouldn't be home for Christmas. The bedside telephone rang and I answered. It was Carol's mum, Rose. Sensing this might be a good time to take my leave, I spent a few moments confirming arrangements to pick her up for a hospital visit on Christmas morning. I passed the phone to Carol. Another kiss, a Merry Christmas, a wave goodbye, and I fled the room before Carol saw the sadness in my eyes. Home I went to our empty apartment.

I poured myself a drink and then, after a moment's hesitation, plugged in the extension cord and lit the tree. Sitting there in the glow of the lights, my one drink led to another, and another, and by the time I called Carol for a final goodnight my mood was maudlin, to say the least.

It wasn't much of a conversation. I got out the words, "Hi honey, how are you feeling?" and then listened as the sound of muffled sobbing reached me through the earpiece. I tried to comfort her, promising to arrive with her mother first thing Christmas morning, but my words had little effect. I closed with a silly suggestion about getting to sleep or Santa wouldn't come and then gently replaced the receiver, before my voice cracked.

"Wait a minute! Santa Claus!" My thoughts started to race.

"Why not?" I said to myself. "It just might work!"

Being an elementary school teacher has its creative

advantages. Hanging in our hall closet was the borrowed Santa suit I'd worn in my school's Christmas concert. I downed my drink and started dressing, shivering with excitement as I suited up, beard and all. Realizing (by some gift of grace) that driving myself was out of the question, I called a cab. I selected several packages from under the tree for my Santa sack and then headed down to the lobby for pick-up.

The cab driver was only mildly surprised. I suspect delivering not-so-sober Santas on Christmas Eve was not entirely out of his realm of experience. I confirmed my destination as the hospital and we set off. During the fifteen minute trip I briefed him on my mission, but the more I talked I'm afraid the sillier my plan sounded. The cabby was sympathetic though, and even got into the spirit of things.

"Look," he said, "I know this place. The main entrance is locked at this time of night and you'll never get past the desk in Emergency. But the shift changes at midnight and the nurses' entrance off the back parking lot will be open. I know. That's where I drop them off and pick them up. In fact when I got the call for a hospital run I thought you were a nurse going in for work; until I saw the get-up that is."

We turned into the driveway. Soldiers' Memorial was built in a U shape, with the main and Emergency entrances at the points of the U. The wings extended forward on either side of a central square, which was dominated by a storeys-tall spruce. Cloaked in a Christmas card mantle of snow, it was decorated for the festive season with strings of red and green lights and topped with a brilliant star. The cabby bypassed the circular front driveway and pulled around to the rear of the building. Sure enough, there was the staff entrance. In fact, a taxi was just pulling away, and its passenger, bundled against the chill and wearing a nurse's cap, was entering the door. The cab slowed to a halt and I reached for my wallet.

"Oh, oh!"

In my haste to get dressed, I had neglected to bring my wallet. But it appears that Santa has little use for money in any event, because the suit lacked pockets. As I patted my outfit in a futile search for funds, the cabby gave me a knowing smile.

"Look," he said, "nobody would make up a story like this just to get out of a cab fare. Tell you what. Here's my card. Our dispatch office is just up the street. When you get your act together, drop the money off there. Good luck and wish her a Merry Christmas for me. And remember, I know where you live."

I glanced at the card for his name. "Thanks Frank," I said; "I won't forget."

I tucked the card into the top of my boot, shook his hand and gave him my best, "Merry Christmas!"

After struggling out of the back seat I slung the toy bag over my shoulder, mounted the steps and cautiously entered the building. The coast was clear and I began to climb, heading for Carol's room on the fourth floor. I was as nervous as a long-tailed cat in a roomful of rocking chairs. The sound of my own breathing rasped in my ears as I tiptoed cautiously upward, straining to avoid detection. I stepped on to the landing between the third and fourth floors and . . .

"So you see officer, I've just got to get in to see her."

"All right, all right, I get the idea," he said. "The least I can do is check it out. Come on, let's go." He motioned at me with the flashlight, ushering me up to the next landing and through the door into the surgical ward.

"What have we here, Art?" said a familiar voice.

There stood Nurse Krause.

"Not the real Santa Claus, that's for sure!" replied the guard. "Says his name is Forrest and claims his wife is in this ward. I caught him sneaking up the back stairs."

Krause reached over, lifted the cap from my head and peeked under my whiskers.

"Well, so it is!" she said, releasing my beard and replacing the cap.

"Mr. Forrest, what are you doing here? I thought I told you to go home and get some sleep?"

"I did," I replied bravely, "and now I'm back. I couldn't leave Carol alone here tonight."

"She's not alone," said Krause stonily. "I'm here."

"But you don't understand; this is—"

Krause cut me off. "Oh yes I do. She's been crying on my shoulder ever since I came back on duty. Your first Christmas together and her birthday. Imagine, trying to get me to help convince the doctor to let her go home tomorrow. Now take me. I'm working a double shift: tonight and tomorrow. You don't hear me complaining, do you?"

Her look, however, softened a little. She turned to the security guard and said resignedly, "Okay Art, leave him with me. I'll look after this. Merry Christmas, and watch your step on those stairs."

Art shuffled off to continue his rounds and Nurse Krause and I were left alone, facing each other over the counter of the nursing station.

"You look ridiculous!" she said, and then wrinkling her nose she added, "Have you been drinking, Mr. Forrest?"

"Well, just a little," I admitted. "I was lonely, so I had a few at home and then I got this crazy idea to dress up as Santa and visit Carol."

"So I see, and now here you are. Well, you're lucky. I just checked your wife's room and she's still awake, feeling sorry for herself. She might as well have some company."

My face brightened. "You mean . . ."

"Come along," said Krause curtly, "and don't make any noise with those boots!"

The door to room 404 was open. Carol lay on her back, staring at the ceiling. The glow from the lights on the tree in the courtyard filtered through the drapes, softly lighting the room. At the sound of my footsteps she turned her head toward the door. "Santa?" she said.

"Merry Christmas!" I replied.

"John, what are you doing here!" she exclaimed, as she struggled to sit up in bed, wincing with pain at the effort.

"That's exactly what I said when the security guard delivered him to me," interjected Krause.

"Can he stay?" asked Carol.

I put on my most mournful expression and hung my head a little.

"Well, now that he's here, he might as well stay. But

not for long," she allowed, as she exited.

"Thanks Krause, Merry Christmas!" called Carol.

I gave her a quick peck on the forehead and then pulled up a chair.

"How did you . . ." she started.

"Later," I said. "Let's open some presents!"

I flopped the toy bag on my lap, loosened the drawstring, selected a package and passed it to her. "Here, I brought one for your birthday and one each for Christmas. We can open these tonight and I'll bring the rest up tomorrow."

Carol opened her present first and found a pair of very small diamond earrings nestled in a blue velvet box. After some suitable oohing and ahhing and a struggle with the I.V. line, she managed to put them in. They looked great. I opened mine next and discovered the sports-watch I had been hoping for. Slipping it on my wrist, I held it out for us both to admire. I left my chair and sat carefully on the side of her bed. Leaning forward, I took Carol gently by the shoulders and . . .

"Okay you two, that's enough of that," said Krause, as she swept into the room pushing a wheelchair.

"You, Santa, have got to get going—right now!"

"All right," I replied reluctantly; "just let us finish opening this . . ."

"You too Mrs. Claus; let's go," continued Krause. With that she lifted the I.V. bottle off the bed frame and rehung it on the support pole attached to the wheelchair. Then she assisted Carol off the bed and seated her.

"All right, now move it!" She wheeled Carol out of the room.

I grabbed my Santa hat, clapped it on my head and followed Krause on her way to the nursing station. There sat a large laundry cart, filled to overflowing with wrapped presents and assorted stuffed toys.

"Let's go Santa, you've got a job to do," barked Krause.

"What?" I said. "Go where?"

"Paediatrics," she replied. "The children's ward; it's just down the hall. Who better to deliver their gifts? You push the cart and I'll push Mrs. Claus." With that she produced another red cap and placed it on Carol's head.

"Now move out!" She motioned toward the end of the hall. Down the corridor we went, Santa in the lead with his mobile toy box and Mrs. Claus behind, with Krause the elf pushing her chair. One of the big double doors at the entrance to Paeds swung open and another nurse met us.

"Merry Christmas Krause!" she said.

"Merry Christmas Nurse Boyd," replied Krause. "As you can see I have some help this year."

"Merry Christmas Santa, and . . . ah, Mrs. Claus," added Boyd.

We got busy.

Each of the rooms had four beds and most were occupied with small bodies, curled into every conceivable position for sleep. As we moved from room to room Boyd checked tags, selected the appropriate present and passed it to me. I tiptoed from bed to bed placing the gifts inside the rails with their occupants, while Carol and Krause hung candy canes in strategic locations. At first I was nervous. Every change of position or muffled cough gave me a start, but I soon became comfortable with my role. After all what else would Santa Claus be doing on Christmas Eve? Room after room and present after present; even Carol had a smile on her face. By the time we reached our final stop I found I was thoroughly enjoying myself.

"Well Krause, who's next?" I asked.

"Robbie," she replied softly.

"Okay, what have we got for him?"

"Nothing special, just a stuffed toy," she said. "He only came in this afternoon; car accident victim and . . ." She broke off.

"Is he badly hurt?" I asked.

"Well, not really. He's got a slight concussion and some cuts and bruises. He's going to be all right."

"That's good," I said.

Krause continued, "Not entirely Mr. Forrest. His parents didn't fare as well. His father was killed. His mother is in a coma. She's in the intensive care room, next to your wife's."

Suddenly I wasn't so sure I wanted to go into that last room.

"Does he . . ."

"He knows," said Krause. "He saw the ambulance crew working on his dad in the wreckage. He heard them when they called the code and gave up the fight to save him. He knows and he seems to have accepted it, or maybe it just hasn't hit him yet. It's his mother he's worried about. He knows she's alive, but he's afraid she won't ever wake up and he'll lose her too."

Boyd handed me the last present. It was a teddy bear. I crept forward with the gift in my hand. Robbie was the sole occupant of the room. He was lying on his back, ramrod straight, covered by a single sheet. The drapes were open and his upper body was bathed in the glow from the lights on the courtyard tree. He looked to be about six years old. There was a bandage on his forehead that dipped down to cover his left eye. I reached over the railing to place the bear beside him. His right eye blinked open.

"Santa!" said Robbie.

"Ah . . . Hi Robbie," I said.

"What are you doing at the hospital?" he asked.

I struggled to form a reply. "Well, uhmm, after I finish visiting all the houses and apartments I come here to make sure the children who can't be at home tonight get a present."

I paused for a moment and then added, "Shouldn't you be asleep? I can't get my last minute deliveries done if boys and girls are still awake."

"I'm sorry Santa. I've being trying to go to sleep but I just can't."

"That's okay," I replied. "Here, I'll tell you what. You snuggle down, hold on to Teddy here and close your eyes."

"Okay Santa, I'll try." Robbie gathered the bear into his chest and closed his eye. However, I could tell from the sound of his voice that Santa's visit hadn't done much to raise his spirits. I backed away from the bed and was turning to leave when Robbie's voice stopped me.

"Santa, can you grant wishes?"

I thought for a moment and then answered.

"Well Robbie, Santa tries to make everyone's Christmas wish come true, but sometimes my elves just can't make enough of some toys and I have to leave something else."

"But your elves don't have to make what I want for Christmas, Santa. I just really want my mum to wake up."

"Well Santa," I thought, "what now?" Suddenly this job wasn't quite so easy. I glanced across the bed at Krause who was tucking in Robbie's covers. Her reply to my silent plea for help was a slight shake of her head. I was still mentally reaching for an answer to Robbie's question when the light from the tree in the courtyard caught my eye.

"Robbie," I asked, "can you see the star on the top of that tree?"

Robbie turned his head toward the window and nodded. "Yes Santa."

"Well Robbie, Santa can't make every wish come true, but that star is a symbol of the hopes and wishes and prayers of people all around the world. It represents the star that the Wise Men followed to find the baby Jesus. They believed and their wish came true. Maybe if you believe and hope, your wish will come true."

Robbie smiled up at us. "Thank you Santa," he said softly, "I'll try." Then he snuggled down under the covers, turned his head toward the window and fixed his gaze on the brilliant white star that topped the courtyard tree.

Krause ushered us out of the room and the door sighed shut.

"John, you shouldn't have told him that!" said Carol.

"What else could I do?" I answered. "I had to say something."

"It's all right," said Krause. "When all else fails

sometimes hope is the best medicine. Come on, let's get Mrs. Claus here back to her room."

We set off down the hall in the direction of the surgical ward. Boyd ushered us back through the doors with a "Thanks Santa, and Merry Christmas!" We replied in kind and wheeled Carol toward her room. As we passed room 402 the door swung open and a nurse exited. I caught a glimpse of a woman lying motionless in the bed. A maze of tubes and wires ran from her body to an assortment of monitors and I could hear a regular beeping in the background.

"Robbie's mum?" I asked Krause.

"Yes," nodded Krause, "that's her."

"Will she recover?" said Carol.

"We just don't know," answered Krause. "Head injuries are very unpredictable. She should have regained consciousness by now, but hasn't. The main concern is how long she'll stay in the coma. The longer she's unconscious, the poorer the chances of a complete recovery." Then she added, "But there's always hope. Right Santa?"

We pulled into Carol's room and rolled to a stop. Krause transferred the I.V. bottle back to the bed frame and we both helped Carol into bed. Delivering the presents had done much to restore our Christmas spirit and though we had been sobered by our final visit, it had served to put our problems in perspective. We were both tired. I checked my new watch: 1:30 a.m. It was Christmas Day.

"Merry Christmas honey," I said, "and happy birthday too!"

"Merry Christmas!" replied Carol.

I gave her hand a soft squeeze and then stood back as Krause finished tucking her in.

"Okay Santa, on your way," said Krause. "Your work here is done for the night."

She escorted me to the door and turned off the light. The bed was once again washed in soft hues of colour from the tree in the hospital square. Carol lay flat on her back, legs slightly raised and bulging the covers, but her head was turned toward the window, her gaze fixed on the Christmas star. I followed Krause back to the nursing station and waited dutifully as she called down to Security for Art.

"Can't have you wandering around by yourself," she said. "You never know what you'd get into."

Art arrived and took me into custody. We boarded the elevator together and descended to the main lobby.

"Well, any luck?" he asked. "Did you get in to visit your wife?"

I filled him in on what had happened and he chuckled. "Good old Krause. She's still at it I see."

"What do you mean?"

Art explained. "Krause came here about ten years ago. She worked in the kids' ward for the first nine years and each year she'd volunteer to double shift: Christmas Eve and Christmas Day. She said it was for the overtime, but we knew differently. Most of the nurses in Paeds have kids of their own and appreciate the time off to be with them."

"What about her family?" I asked.

Art shrugged, "Nobody knows. Oh, there're stories about a son that died and a broken marriage, but they're just stories. What I do know is that every Christmas she organizes presents for the children who have to stay in the hospital. The parents leave a gift with her for delivery to their kids and if that isn't possible Krause always seems to come up with some extras to go around. Nobody misses out on their visit from Santa. She was transferred out of Paediatrics earlier this year, but it looks as if she's been able to keep up the tradition anyway and even add to it, with your help."

The elevator door opened onto the lobby of Emergency and Art escorted me over to the bank of taxi phones.

"Merry Christmas Art, and thanks," I said as he left me.

I reached down, retrieved Frank's card from my boot top and then lifted his company's receiver. A dispatcher answered and I requested a cab, asking for Frank if he was available. He was, and after a short wait his car pulled up to the door. I climbed into the front this time.

"Well Santa, how did it go?"

"Great Frank; things were a little sticky at first but everything worked out in the end. Carol's feeling better and we even did a little work on Santa's behalf." I went on to tell him about Krause and the delivery of the presents. I left out the part about Robbie.

We pulled into the driveway in front of our apartment building. "Wait here for a minute, will you Frank? I'll be right back." I hurried up to our apartment, recovered my wallet and slipped back down to pay my combined $12.00 fare. I handed him a twenty.

"Keep the change," I said. "You earned it."

"Thanks Santa, and Merry Christmas to you too."

Back upstairs I went. Once inside I stripped off my

Santa outfit, plugged in the tree lights and lay down on the couch. The last thing I remember was focusing on our tree top star and making my own wish.

I awoke to the insistent ringing of the telephone behind me on the end table. It was Carol's mum with my wake up call. I glanced at the clock: 8:00 a.m. I thanked Rose for calling, placed my breakfast order and gave her my timeline for pick-up.

I made it to her house thirty minutes later, gobbled down my bacon and eggs and we set out for the hospital, arriving a little before 10:00 a.m.

"Good morning Santa . . . I mean Mr. Forrest," said Krause. I introduced Carol's mum and then asked Krause for an update on Carol's condition.

"See for yourselves," she replied.

We were pleasantly surprised when we entered the room. Carol was seated on the edge of the bed, clad in a housecoat and slippers, resplendent in her new earrings. The I.V. had been removed. She looked great, considering her surgery had been less than 48 hours earlier, and there was a smile on her face. We exchanged Christmas and birthday greetings. Rose joined her on the bed and delivered a motherly hug. Carol told us about Doctor Robinson's visit a half an hour earlier, his order to remove the I.V. and his non-committal reply to her plea to be released. Rose joked about the Christmas she missed while giving birth to Carol and we surprised her with the story of our Christmas Eve adventure. We were about to begin opening the presents we'd brought with us when Krause appeared in the doorway.

"Mr. Forrest, I'll have to ask you to excuse us," she said.

"Aw Krause, can't it wait until after we open the presents?" I pleaded.

"Now see here you! Just because I felt sorry for you last night doesn't mean you can get away with anything today. You can open them later. Besides, I have to change her dressing before she goes home and I can't do that with you here."

"What did you say?" blurted Carol. "Did you say home?" she squeaked, as her eyes filled with tears. "I'm going home today? Really?"

"That's right," said Krause, "as soon as we can get you out the door. When Doctor Robinson stopped by after rounds, he wanted to know how you were really doing. I think your tale of woe had him pretty well convinced, but when I told him about last night and added that if he didn't let you out today I'd probably have to put in a cot for your husband, he decided that home would be the best place for you both. Besides, we need this bed for another patient. So you"—she pointed at me—"out! Mrs. Pearce, you can stay and start packing Carol's things, while I change her dressing."

With that Krause hustled me to the door and out into the hallway. "If you want to make yourself useful you can go and get a wheelchair." She pointed down the hall toward Paediatrics and then ducked back into the room, closing the door behind her.

"All right!" I cried, as I clapped my hands together. "What a great Christmas present!" There was some extra spring in my step as I set off to acquire a chair.

As I passed Room 402 I noticed the door was open. I glanced in to check on Rob's mum. My heart skipped a beat. The bed was empty. In fact, a blue clad member of the housekeeping staff was stripping the bedclothes, while her partner was beginning to wash down the frame. I had enough hospital experience to know what that meant.

"Oh no," I thought, "not his mum too!"

Suddenly our good fortune seemed out of place.

The wheelchair we'd used last night was gone from its parking spot and I couldn't see another one. The entrance to Paeds was right there.

"Maybe I can borrow one from them," I thought. I pushed through the door.

Talk about Christmas spirit. The corridor was full of kids. Some were trying out their new toys and others were being moved about in wheelchairs. A doctor hustled past, stethoscope in hand and sporting a pair of clip-on reindeer antlers. The noise level was anything but hospital-like. I spotted one or two of the stuffed toys we had handed out the night before and I recognized some of the kids too, I think. I searched the crowd for a boy with a bandaged head and eye, hoping to catch sight of Robbie, but he was nowhere to be seen. Boyd was still on duty.

"Merry Christmas Nurse Boyd!"

"Santa," she replied, "shouldn't you be resting today?"

"How's Robbie?" I asked.

"See for yourself," she said, and pointed toward the open door to his room. Then, dodging a speeding wind-up car, she went on about her duties. I approached the door to Robbie's room and peered cautiously in. Robbie was sitting on the edge of his bed, legs dangling and kicking, arms gesturing in support of his words. Sitting in a wheelchair beside the bed, holding the teddy bear in her lap, was his mother. I could hear the excitement in his voice.

"Santa brought him. He was right here last night. He talked to me. He really did! I asked him for a wish, to help you wake up and he told me about the star of hope." He pointed toward the window. "And I did hope and my wish came true, just like Santa said."

I couldn't hear his mother's soft reply, but I did see her hands tighten on the stuffed toy and the tear that trickled from the corner of her eye.

I felt a tap on my shoulder. It was Krause. She motioned me away from the door.

"When?" I asked.

"She came out of it about an hour after you left."

"And ...?" I prompted.

"She's going to be fine. She'll be here for a few more days while we run some tests, but the two of them should be out of here before New Year's. In fact, we're moving her into Carol's room. That's one of the reasons she's getting out of here today. Speaking of Carol, she's ready to go. Are you?"

We headed back to the surgical ward, arriving at about the same time as an orderly with the needed wheelchair. He and Krause helped Carol into the chair while her mum and I gathered up the unopened presents and the suitcase.

Our entourage made its way to the elevator. While we waited for a car I updated Carol on Robbie and his mum and, although I didn't think it possible, her smile seemed to get even brighter.

"That's wonderful!" she said. "It looks like all of our Christmas wishes have come true."

The doors pulled open and we boarded. I held the car for a moment longer. I looked down at Carol and then we both looked back to Krause.

"Merry Christmas!" we said together.

"Merry Christmas, you two," replied Krause, "and thanks again for your help last night."

Carol smiled up at me from the chair and squeezed my hand.

"It's you who helped us Krause," she said softly.

The doors slid shut and we were on our way home for Christmas.

That Special Tree

"Johnnie? John!"

The sharp tone of the teacher's voice pierced my thoughts and the vision of the family gathered around the Christmas tree in their wilderness cabin faded quickly from my mind. Although our Friday afternoon story time was over, I had remained caught in the author's magic web. Grinning sheepishly, I ducked my head and rummaged in my desk, ears burning at the sound of giggling from my grade two classmates.

With the approach of the holidays, Miss Campbell had been reading a story about a pioneer family's Christmas. In their struggle to get ready for their first winter in the Canadian north, they had forgotten all about celebrating the season. All but one of them that is! The youngest child, a boy about my age, slips away on a special mission. When they discover he's missing, his worried family fears the worst, but our hero returns home safely, dragging a beautiful evergreen up to the door of the cabin. It was the stuff that dreams are made of!

The bell rang and Miss Campbell dismissed us, but I hung back to avoid the teasing I knew I would face in the cloakroom. I noticed my friend Jim was also taking his time and I smiled my thanks to him. We struggled into our heavy winter clothing, slipped out the door and headed for the gate at the far end of the playground.

"You know, I really liked that story too!" said Jim.

"You did?" I asked.

"Sure," he replied. "That kid must have felt so neat when he brought the tree home."

"Yeah, and his family was so proud of him!" I added. "What a great way to feel at Christmas!"

We continued to scuff our way through the ankle deep snow, down the path that was the shortcut to our houses.

"Have you got your tree yet?" I asked.

"No," he answered. "How about you?"

"Nah; we usually wait until the Saturday before Christmas to get ours."

"You know," remarked Jim, "it's too bad we couldn't get our own trees, just like the kid in the story."

I stopped dead in my tracks and looked right at him. "Why not?" I said.

"Where would we get a tree?" he scoffed.

"Well look around." I swung my arm in a pointing arc. "There's lots of them in these woods."

"Yeah, but they're not real Christmas trees; they're scraggly!"

I persisted, "There's plenty of pines around here. We

can look for just the right ones tomorrow."

"Sure, but even if we did find some, how would we cut them down and get them home?"

"No problem, I'll get Dad's limb saw and we can use your toboggan to haul them. What do you think?"

"Okay," he said, "let's do it! I'll meet you tomorrow morning at Fudger's Pond."

With that, Jim climbed the fence and dropped into his backyard. I continued on my way home, eyes straining to scan the bush in the gathering dusk, hoping to spot that special tree.

Saturday morning dawned crisp and clear, with a light dusting of new snow sprinkled on the landscape. Fudger's Pond was frozen over and Jim was testing the sliding while he waited for me. With him towing the toboggan and me shouldering the saw, we started our search for those perfect pines. Every flash of green caught our eye and we hurried from tree to tree, trying to pick the best ones. Each time we thought we had discovered the right tree, we would find a flaw. Too short, too tall, too thin, too this, too that—and of course, there was always a better looking tree, "Just over there!"

Unfortunately, the trees we were finding were not real Christmas trees. They looked good from a distance, but when we got up close they turned out to be poor imitations of the excellent evergreens we wanted. These scrawny firs and sickly cedars just wouldn't do! Our enthusiasm was beginning to wane and our boots started to drag through the snow. We stopped to rest and talk things over.

"I can't believe," I said, "that none of these trees are any good!"

"Me neither," puffed Jim. "There must be some real Christmas trees around here somewhere!"

We flopped in the snow and nibbled on a few handfuls of the white stuff, while we considered our next move.

"I know! What about the laneway up behind the golf course? Remember when we rode our bikes down there last summer? I'm sure I saw some trees. Good ones too!"

Jim thought for a minute, then struggled to his feet, dusted off the snow and grabbed the rope to his toboggan. "Come on," he said; "let's go!"

I hitched the saw a little higher on my shoulder and we set out across country, toward our new goal. The going was tough and by the time we got to the back road that ran beside the golf course our seven-year-old legs were tiring; but we kept on until we reached the entrance to the laneway. Two imposing fieldstone pillars guarded the Rattray Estate, but the gate was open. We clambered over the small bank of snow blocking our way and surveyed the sloping lane. Its icy wheel ruts made a perfect toboggan track. It was time to have some fun!

I tucked the saw under the seat pad. Jim hopped on, I pushed off and then piled on behind him. We slid down the slope, gathering speed like a bobsled. Too much speed!

We rocketed into the curve at the bottom of the hill. Our toboggan jumped the track, climbed a snowbank and dumped us into a drift! I rolled out of the wreckage, brushed off the flakes and looked around to get my bearings. There before me, cloaked in Christmas-card mantles of snow, stood our trees!

"Look at them!" gasped Jim.

"Wow!" I cried. "They're perfect!"

We scrambled to our feet and raced up the road to get a closer look. The trees maintained their perfection, even under our close and now critical scrutiny. They stood like sentinels, one on each side of the driveway, leading to the group of buildings on the hill above. We selected our target and burrowed under its bottom branches, discovering a secret, silent world, sheltered from the elements, safe and secure. Our eyes adjusted to the eerie half-light and we studied the trunk. It seemed huge, as thick as my leg. But no matter; I wanted that tree!

I started to cut, but it was not easy. The saw was hard to handle and it was very difficult to get its large teeth to bite. After several failed attempts, Jim and I settled on the lumberjack method, each of us on an end, pushing and pulling. We made some progress, but it was slow going. The weight of the tree kept causing the saw to stick and our frustration grew. We stopped to rest.

"We'll never cut through this trunk!" Jim complained.

"Not today anyway," I agreed, "but we've got until next week to finish the job."

We got back to work, but hunger and weariness were beginning to take their toll. Jim poked his head out of our nest and noted the late afternoon sun dipping toward the horizon.

"We'd better head for home," he said.

We left the saw hidden under the tree and trudged wearily, but happily, toward our houses, parting company only after planning to meet the next afternoon.

When I got home I answered Mum's usual questions about my day with a casual, "Ah, just messing around with Jim, tobogganing at the golf course."

I don't think Mum and Dad were suspicious, but I'm sure they were surprised when, shortly after dinner, I headed off to bed voluntarily! I slept soundly, brightly lit Christmas trees glowing in my dreams.

Jim and I met at the golf course just after lunch on Sunday. We hurried to the trees and got right to work on his. Now experienced woodsmen, we had better success. By late afternoon, both trees were ready to fall and we stopped to plan.

"Should we finish them off?" asked Jim.

"Let's wait," I suggested. "We can drop them after school on Friday, and take them home with us at dinner."

As we hurried home, our footsteps were light with anticipation.

The days of that last week crept by like snails. The Christmas concert came and went. Carol singing and gift exchanges marked the final Friday before the holidays. We said our classroom goodbyes and dressed quickly. At the sound of the dismissal bell Jim and I bolted out the door, raced home to change and then headed for our trees.

First one and then the other, we finished our cutting and our prizes toppled. Now to get them home!

Transporting our treasures was a real challenge. Using the toboggan we dragged them, one at a time, up the hill to the road. Puffing and panting we knew the worst was over, but darkness was falling and we were still a long way from home. Jim towed his tree on the toboggan and I skidded mine along the snow-covered shoulder of the road. Cars slid past, flashing their lights in the gathering dusk while giving our procession a wide berth. The street lamps blinked on. Strings of Christmas lights began to twinkle on the houses and a gentle snow started to fall. It was a storybook scene. Jim and I paused before we split up.

"Well, we did it!" he boasted.

"We sure did!" I agreed.

With smiles lighting our faces we called, "Merry Christmas!" and went our separate ways.

I was very late and I knew Mum would be worried, but delivering "The Tree" would make everything all right. The front of our house was bathed in red and green by the floodlights on the lawn. The car was in the driveway. Dad was already home from work!

I rested the tree against the front porch, rang the bell and then stood down proudly, beside my gift. Mum opened the storm door and peered out. A look of relief crossed her face, followed quickly by one of surprise and then concern.

"John!" she exclaimed, "where did you get that tree?"

"Do you like it?" I asked.

Dad appeared behind her, took one look at my tree, put his hand to his forehead and muttered, "Oh no."

My heart sank! This was not the reaction I had expected.

"What's wrong?" I stammered, my voice breaking.

"Do you know what that is?" Mum queried.

"It's our Christmas tree!" I replied. "I cut it just for us. I thought you'd like it," I squeaked, my eyes filling with tears.

Dad came to the rescue.

"We do son, we do," he said, nudging Mum.

"Come inside and get warm and tell us all about it."

I brightened a little and hurried up the steps. Mum stopped me on the way by, hugged me hard and whispered, "It's a wonderful tree dear."

Dinner was warming in the oven and we sat down to eat right away. During the meal, I poured out the story of the wilderness family and my search for just the right tree for our home. When I described where I found ours, another look of concern flashed across mother's face, but it turned quickly to a tight smile.

"Well, what's done is done," said Dad, as he rose from the table.

"You finish eating John. I have some calls to make."

He returned a few minutes later, smiled and nodded at Mum and then tapped me on the shoulder.

"Come on son," he said, "let's put your tree up."

The snow was still falling and the tree was shrouded in white. Dad stood it straight, shook it clean and we sized it up. Working in the soft glow of the floodlights, we trimmed the lower branches, shortened the trunk and clamped on the stand. While we worked, I asked "Dad, what's wrong with my tree?"

"Nothing John," he said. "Ah . . . it's just that it's . . . ah . . . a *very* special tree."

We finished our task. Dad took the butt of the tree and backed in through the door, while I lifted and guided the top. We placed it carefully in the window corner. Perfectly shaped, thick, bushy and tinged with blue, it almost touched the ceiling. We strung the lights and hung the decorations. Dad topped it with a star and Mum and I added the finishing touches of tinsel.

"Okay John, it's your honour," said Dad. "You got the tree; now you light it!"

I grasped the plug in both hands and pressed it into the socket. The tree was transformed into a shimmering cone of multicoloured light. It was magical.

My chest swelled with pride. I swallowed the lump in my throat; "Merry Christmas," I said softly.

"Merry Christmas," replied Mum and Dad.

That was the last time I provided the family Christmas tree. It wasn't until I was older and my parents began telling the story to friends that I fully understood the reason for their reluctant response to my gift. Now, retelling the story of "John's Special Tree" has become a family Christmas tradition.

You see, I had presented my parents with a beautiful blue spruce, which just happened to be one of the matching markers that flanked the driveway of the Rattray Estate. Dad's calls that night were to Jim's parents to verify my story and to the estate's owners, to explain the mysterious disappearance of their perfectly matched trees.

The Rattrays were very understanding. They settled for an apology and a promise that Jim and I would help replace the trees. Late the next summer we revisited the scene of our adventure and spent a day helping the groundskeeper remove the stumps and plant new spruces.

Jim moved away that fall and our paths have not crossed since. But to this day the sight of a blue spruce, frosted with snow, brings back to me images of our childhood quest. And I fondly recall how a very special tree filled a little boy's heart with joy and provided our family with a cherished Christmas memory.

The Gift of Time

—as told to the author
by Carol (Pearce) Forrest

It had been a wonderful Christmas morning. Santa Claus had been very good to my sister Gail and me, and the fact that I was a Christmas baby and today was my tenth birthday made it extra special. After opening our presents and eating Christmas "brunch" with Mum and Dad, Gail and I scooted upstairs to our bedroom to try out some of our gifts. She was placing another stack of 45s on the spindle of the record player and I was about to model another of my new sweaters when Mum called up to us.

"Carol! Gail! Are you two dressed yet? We're leaving soon to visit your grandmother. You can wear the outfits that you got for Christmas. Hurry up, she's expecting us soon!"

Gail and I exchanged pained looks. Now don't get me wrong; we loved our Gramma White dearly, but having to visit a nursing home on Christmas Day was not our idea of fun. The first record dropped onto the turntable and our consciences were prodded as the mournful melody of Elvis's Blue Christmas issued from the speaker. We shrugged our shoulders in joint resignation and started to get dressed.

Gramma White had been living with us for the past three years, but a month ago she had fallen on the stairs and broken her hip. During her hospital stay, Dad and Mum held a family conference and explained that Gramma would not be coming home again. She needed greater care, both physically and mentally, than we could provide in our home. So when she was ready to be released from the hospital, she was placed in a nursing home on Senlac Road, just a few blocks away from our house on Lorraine Drive. Mum visited her almost every day.

Gail and I had dropped in to say hello a few times on our way home from school. The white metal beds and side tables were all the same and everything else was painted in varying shades of pale green. Gramma usually remembered who were, but some times she didn't and we would coax her into conversation by talking about the old days at the cottage. The dry air was always too warm and seemed stale and tainted with the odours of illness and aging. I felt uncomfortable standing next to her bed in a large room filled with other "old" people and our visits were usually very short.

Christmas had always been Gramma's favourite time of year. But over the past few weeks, as the staff hung decorations and the radio played Christmas carols,

Gramma became aware that this would be her first Christmas away from home and family; she grew very sad. To cheer her up we told her we would bring Christmas to her. It was time to keep our promise.

Gail and I came downstairs to the kitchen where Mum approved our skirt, blouse and matching red sweater outfits and put the finishing touches on our hair. Dad had already loaded the presents and was warming up the car. It was just a five-minute drive to the home. The sky was overcast but an early morning snowfall had given the neighbourhood a fresh and festive look. Gail and I carried the presents while Dad got the doors and we entered the lobby of the three-story red brick building. The communal Christmas tree was lighted and there were decorations taped to the walls but the hallways were empty of people and our footsteps echoed hollowly in the stairwell as we made our way to the second floor. When we walked passed the long line of beds in the ward I noticed most of the patients were sleeping and that we seemed to be the only visitors.

Gramma was sitting up in bed and when she saw us she smiled broadly and responded happily to our hugs and Merry Christmas wishes. She was having a good day!

We gathered around her and had a wonderful time: opening gifts, telling tales of Christmas past and even singing carols. Gramma was thrilled and her spirits had clearly been lifted.

But Dad too had noticed that few of the other patients had visitors. While we continued to chat with Gramma, he remained quiet and seemed deep in thought. Then he excused himself and left the ward. When he returned a little while later, he was carrying three cartons of ice cream "Dixie Cups" from the cafeteria.

Dad explained his plan. Christmas was a time for family and celebrating the joys of the season together with our loved ones. If for whatever reason family and friends couldn't be there for some of the other patients, then we would substitute and bring the spirit of Christmas to them too. So, while Mum stayed with Gramma, the three of us went visiting. Dad took Gail and me across the hall and explained our mission to the nurse, who was more than happy to assist. Dad went back to do his visiting in Gramma's ward and the nurse got Gail and me started on opposite sides of her ward.

A shy ten-year-old, I was very nervous at first. I didn't know any of these people and sadly some of them were a little confused and even uncertain about what was so special about this particular day. The nurse escorted me to the bedside of my first challenge and pointed out the patient's name on a sign taped at the foot of her bed. After a moment's hesitation, I summoned the courage to introduce myself and offer her some ice cream. Although the memory of her name has faded over the years, I still recall her warm greeting. She declined the treat, but smiled and said "Hello Carol, I have a granddaughter about your age. She lives out west and she won't be able to visit me this year. I bet you two have a lot in common. Sit down and tell me what you got for Christmas."

That first successful stop helped me overcome my stage fright and as I moved from bed to bed the heart-warming smiles and kind comments that resulted from each visit gave me confidence. I really began to get into the spirit of things. I especially remember my last stop. I had just two cups of ice cream left and I was saving one of them for myself.

The occupant of that final bed was a very frail looking woman. A halo of soft white hair framed her heavily lined face and her head was sunk deep in the pillow. She appeared to be asleep. I sat in the chair beside her bed and said softly, "Merry Christmas. Would you like some ice cream?"

Her eyelids fluttered and then opened wide revealing a pair of bright blue eyes. She frowned, then fixed her gaze on me.

"But," she said hesitantly, "I don't have any money."

"That's okay," I replied; "they're free."

"Oh," she said. A bright smile spread across her face, erasing decades of age. "In that case, I'll have two."

I opened both of the ice cream cups, unwrapped the wooden spoon, and passed them to her. I talked, while she ate.

That was almost fifty Christmases ago, but I can still picture those sparkling blue eyes and recall the wonderful feeling that came from giving another person the priceless gift of my time.

The Elves'
Christmas Tree

My mother is very passionate about Christmas and her preparations for the holiday season were always very meticulous. Sometimes her enthusiasm for having everything just so led to excess. Thankfully, such was the case in 1955.

Our family was living in Lorne Park, a small community set on the shore of Lake Ontario about midway between Toronto and Hamilton. My brother Will and I attended Owenwood Public School, he in kindergarten and I in grade 3. That year the Home and School Association decided to sell Christmas Trees as a fundraiser. Families were asked to pre-order their trees, which were to be delivered a few days before Christmas. I'm sure virtually every family bought a tree and every child in the school was eagerly anticipating their arrival.

Monday of the last week before the holiday break

came, but our trees didn't. Tuesday, the same. Wednesday, no trees. Finally, on Thursday, a big truck carrying our trees pulled into the parking lot. Learning came to an abrupt halt as noses were pressed to every classroom window to watch the unloading. Principal Stevens and some boys from the Grade 8 class helped the driver and the trees were piled in the fenced kindergarten yard.

The plan for distribution was simple. That week's art lesson had been devoted to designing and making personal tree tags. The eldest child was given the responsibility of picking out the family's tree and tagging it for pick-up by their parents. I made a large bristol board tag with the name Forrest printed boldly in red on the white background and decorated my creation with colourful illustrations of candy canes and Christmas stars. When Principal Stevens arrived at our classroom door to escort us out to the yard, I could hardly contain myself.

Our teacher dismissed the dozen or so of us that were designated and clutching our tags we accompanied Mr. Stevens to the kindergarten yard to pick out our Yule tree. Of course all of us wanted to pick the best tree for our family.

The responsibility weighed heavily on my shoulders; Mum had carefully instructed me on just what to look for. I was to select a bushy, well-shaped tree with a straight trunk and at least one good side. Many of the trees were already tagged but there were still lots to choose from. I began my quest for the best.

Some parent volunteers were on hand to help by

standing the trees erect and providing advice. It was fun but difficult. The trees were Scotch pines, notorious for having crooked trunks, and came in a wide variety of shapes and sizes. I carefully examined a number and rejected them for various reasons, but I soon found just the right tree. Mum would be pleased. I proudly and carefully affixed my tag and headed back to class.

That night at dinner I told Mum and Dad all about it and loudly proclaimed the merits of the tree I had chosen for us.

I expected that right after eating we would walk up the school to pick up our tree, but I was disappointed. Not knowing that Dad would be called in to work overtime that night, Mum had agreed to look after a neighbour's baby while she went Christmas shopping. I was disappointed, but no matter, our tree was tagged and waiting. We could pick it up tomorrow night.

When I arrived at school the next morning the first thing I did was look for my tree. There it was still leaning up against the fence where I had left it, with my tag clearly proclaiming our ownership. That school day seemed to last forever and at recess and noon I visited the kindergarten yard just to check on it before heading off to play.

But our class party and gift exchange in the afternoon took my mind off things and before I knew it, the dismissal bell rang. Christmas Break had started! I went down to the kindergarten to pick up Will for the walk home and while there I saw a steady stream of parents arriving to pick up their trees, as well as their kids. Our tree was still right where I had left it and I couldn't wait to return with Dad to get it.

As usual, Mum was scrupulous in her Christmas preparations. We even had a schedule to keep to. Under her guidance, in the previous week Dad and I had strung the outdoor lights, set up the manger scene on the lawn and hung the door wreath. She had begun decorating indoors this week. Spray-on snow frosted the inside of our front windowpanes, seasonal candles had been set out and festive garlands and ribbons and bows adorned the mantel and doorways. Even the mistletoe had been hung. The crowning touch would be the raising and decoration of our Christmas tree.

Dad arrived home from work on time and right after dinner he, Will and I set out to get our tree. Bundled against the cold, we took the path from the back of our house through the bush to the schoolyard. Dad held Will's hand and led the way along the snowy path while I followed towing the toboggan that would carry our prized pine home. When we reached the school I could see Mr. Stevens and some of the teachers helping families find and load their trees. I, of course, knew exactly where ours was and I ran straight to it. It was gone!

Dad arrived and questioned me. I stammered out my answer. I didn't know!

Dad calmed me down and suggested we look around to see if, in all the confusion, it had been moved. We walked around the entire yard and inspected each tree, but to no avail. Our tree had disappeared!

Dad decided to ask Mr. Stevens for help while I kept looking. I renewed my search but didn't have to go too far before my fears were verified. There, lying at my feet in the muddy slush, was my tag. Although soggy and smeared with dirt our name was still visible. I scooped it up and ran over and presented it to Dad and Mr. Stevens. They exchanged knowing looks. Someone else had taken our tree. Whether by mistake or not it didn't matter. It was gone. We didn't have a tree and Christmas was only two days away! What would we do? Would Santa still come? This was serious!

Other families continued to haul their trees home for the holidays, while we stood by helpless. As the supply of trees dwindled even Dad started to get agitated. Finally Mr. Stevens came back over to us and, while apologizing profusely, led us to a lone pine, standing in the corner of the yard. He explained that the few extra trees they had ordered had also sold quickly and offered this sole survivor to us. It was a case of take it or leave it. Knowing that Mum was waiting all ready to decorate, Dad wasn't about to return home without a tree. We took it.

Dad helped me load the tree on the toboggan; we wished Mr. Stevens a Merry Christmas and set out for home. On the way Dad suggested we not say anything about the mix-up to Mum. We had a tree and that was all that mattered.

Mum was waiting and welcomed us at the door. She took Will inside with her and Dad and I took the tree into the garage to affix the stand. In the harsh light of the overhead bulb we got our first good look at it. It was not a pretty sight.

Regardless, it was all we had. Dad squared off the

trunk with his saw and then nailed the wooden crosspieces to the butt. We were ready. We carried the tree in through the front door and carefully placed it in the window corner of the living room. Mum had piled the boxes of decorations and lights on the chesterfield ready to be hung. We stepped back too admire our handiwork and I heard Mum gasp.

Our tree was leaning heavily to one side, like a drunk on a binge. The trunk had at least two big twists in it and the branches stuck out at some very odd angles. There were bare spots everywhere! Dad tried turning the tree this way and that, to improve the profile, but it was no use. It wasn't quite a Charlie Brown tree, but it was a great imitation.

At first Mum was speechless and then she started to question me about my choice. I was devastated. I had failed her. I knew it wasn't my fault, but still I felt responsible.

Dad intervened and hastily explained the problem. Noting my distress, Mum unfolded her arms from across her chest; the look on her face softened.

"Well, a tree's a tree," she said. "It's past bedtime for both of you and it's too late now to decorate it and besides, tonight is the last Chimney Inspection Night."

In our family the last few nights before Christmas Eve were designated as Chimney Inspection Nights. This meant that during our single-digit years my little brother Will and I had to be in bed very early and asleep so Santa's Elves could check to be sure we were ready for his visit. But I think they had an arrangement with my parents because invariably Santa's helpers seemed to wait until the night before Christmas Eve to visit. If we passed muster the Elves would leave a candy cane on our bedroom doorknob so we would know that they had visited and Santa would soon follow.

Mum suggested that we have some hot chocolate and save decorating the tree until the morning. Will and I put on our pajamas and returned to the kitchen where we told Mum the tale of our missing tree. We sipped our cocoa, but I'm pretty sure Mum and Dad had something a little stronger. When we headed off to bed, I took one last glance at the tree. I can remember thinking that it looked so bad Santa's Elves might refuse to approve it and he might not even stop at our house this year, let alone leave presents. And it was my fault.

When I got up the next morning I found no candy cane on my doorknob. We had failed inspection! I was heartbroken. As I moped down the hallway to the kitchen I passed the living room and looked in to scowl at the cause of my distress.

There, standing straight and tall in the corner, was the most perfect Christmas tree I had ever seen. Candy canes hung from almost every branch. Something magical had occurred! Then I spotted Mum curled up asleep in the big easy chair. I ran over and woke her to show her what had happened. The Elves had come and they had fixed our tree.

Rubbing the sleep from her eyes she smiled, hugged me hard and agreed with my exclamation that it was the best Christmas tree ever. And it was! Dad wandered in from the kitchen with coffee for two and I ran to get Will out of bed so he could help with the decorating. Christmas that year was wonderful as usual.

I never questioned how the Elves had managed to fix our tree, but once I was old enough to know, Dad told me the real story. Mum had stayed up most of the night saving my tree. First she had hammered some carefully placed nails into the wall and using green twine from her craft basket managed to coax the tree to stand up straight. Next she employed Dad's brace and bit drill to bore strategic holes in the trunk. Then, using branches trimmed from the back of the tree, Mum filled the bare spots, holding her transplanted boughs in place with carpenter's glue and stove pipe wire. She added the final touch using scissors to prune the tree into a perfect shape. I guess you could say that Mum was the inventor of the first "real" artificial Christmas tree.

This year three generations of our family will gather to celebrate and reminisce at Christmas and the story of what is now "The Elves' Christmas Tree" will be recounted. It has been embellished over the years, but fortunately Mum is still with us to supply all the details. And when the children's version of the tale is told, they will of course marvel at the magic of the elves' visit. But I will hear in my heart the real story and remember it fondly as a loving mother's passion to preserve the joy of Christmas for her family.

Oh Christmas Tree!

A *final chorus* of Jingle Bells poured merrily from our throats as we turned into the circular driveway of our apartment building. Our Christmas-tree-laden car slid to a slushy halt in front of the large glass doors leading to the festively decorated lobby and we piled out, laughing and singing with the joy of the season.

The four of us, Ben Hansen and his wife Lynn and my wife Carol and I, were living in the newest high-rise in town, a twelve-story apartment building that was the epitome of urban accommodation for young couples in 1970. We both had balcony suites, the Hansens residing in number 705 and the Forrests in 1005, three floors directly above them.

Today's outing had got our seasonal plans off to a great start. We had spent the morning on a tree farm north of the city, seeking and cutting the perfect pines for our Yuletide celebrations. We had a wonderful time riding on a straw-covered farm sleigh drawn by matching Clydesdales whose jingling bells accompanied our carol singing. Fortified with Christmas cheer from our wineskin we wandered through acres of balsam, spruce and fir, often slogging through knee-deep snow, searching for the best trees. Of course we found them, but now that we had arrived home safely with our prized pines, our next task was to get them up to our apartments and begin decorating. Thank goodness for the elevator.

Ben and I untied the ropes and removed the trees from the roof rack, and while the wives held the entry doors wide we carried them proudly into the lobby. That was as far as we got!

"Where do you think you're going with those?" barked the stern voice of Mrs. Watson, the building superintendent. "Can't you read?" She gestured to the large hand-written sign posted by the elevator, and then recited for our benefit "No Live Christmas Trees Allowed!"

"But we had live trees last year," said Carol.

"That was last year," replied Mrs. Watson. "The building's owners have decided they don't want their carpets and elevators gummed up with pine tar and littered with fallen needles. Besides, they're a fire hazard and a lot of extra work for us!"

It seemed that our superintendents, the elderly husband and wife team of Fred and Edna Watson, were responsible for enforcing this edict and were taking their duty very seriously.

We tried every argument we could muster. We

suggested wrapping the trees in sheets; we promised to clean up afterward. To no avail. Our pleas fell on deaf ears. With Mrs. Watson posted, arms folded, in front of the elevator doors, there was nothing left to do but retreat and discuss strategy. Back outside we went.

After reloading the trees, we drove around to the side of the building and down the ramp into the underground parking garage. Leaving our precious cargo on the car we took the basement elevator up to the Hansens' apartment and held a summit conference. We had a problem to solve; more than one, in fact.

The first was financial. Money was tight and we had budgeted carefully for a real Christmas tree and the lights and ornaments needed to decorate. Not only did we not want an artificial tree, we now couldn't afford one. Second, what were we to do with the trees we already had? There was only one solution. We would sneak them in!

We hatched our plan over bowls of chili and crusts of buttered bread, washed down with bottled Christmas cheer. Ben and I would return to the underground and load the trees on the elevator. Carol would be posted in the lobby to guard against interruption by other tenants or the Watsons. Lynn would take station on the seventh floor ready to receive our delivery. Elevator traffic was usually light in the mid-afternoon, so we synchronised our watches and moved into position at exactly 2:30 p.m. I summoned an elevator car to the underground garage while Ben waited behind a nearby column with our forbidden freight. The door opened, revealing no passengers. I motioned to Ben, stepped back in and held the door open button. He followed swiftly with the tree and somehow managed to cram it and himself into the elevator with me. I closed the door and pressed the button for the seventh floor.

We began our ascent, hearts hammering wildly in our chests, hoping Carol had done her job well. She had. We passed the ground floor without incident and as we reached the 2nd the tension began to drain from my neck and shoulders. I tracked our progress on the lights above the door, 3rd floor, 4th floor, and then . . . the elevator shuddered to a dead stop at the 5th.

Oh, oh! I buried myself in the branches as the door slid open, but Ben was stuck in full view of the waiting passenger, Mr. Watson, who was the other half of the superintendent team. We couldn't get off and he couldn't get on.

"Going down?" asked Ben sheepishly.

"I'm not, but you are!" he replied curtly and then motioned toward me.

I hit the B for basement button and we began our descent to the garage where we returned the tree to the car.

Time for another strategy meeting. We headed back to the Hansens' apartment, picking up Carol on the way, and reported our failure to Lynn. Carol and I returned to our apartment to change clothes and plan dinner. We held our own discussion of the problem but came up with no new solutions. Our plan for that evening had been to spend time in each other's apartments decorating our trees and sipping eggnog, with the soft sounds of seasonal songs playing in the background. Now, without trees, when the Hansens arrived about 7:30 p.m. we poured some drinks and re-opened talks on solving our dilemma. Ben suggested trying to sneak up the stairs but I was leery. Dragging two full-sized Christmas trees up that many flights of stairs would be no mean feat. Plus we would leave a trail of needles leading right to our doors. We even considered trying the elevator again but in those days tenant rights were non-existent and the wives were worried that if we got caught again we would be evicted. We even discussed trying to sell our trees and use the money to purchase artificial ones, but all of our potential customers lived in the building and faced the same restrictions as we did. Besides, we had our hearts set on real trees not imitations that brought to mind a badly assembled collection of green test-tube brushes.

Saturday night was our regular night to play bridge and now, with no trees to decorate, we decided to break out the cards. I was still dealing the first hand when Ben excused himself to use the telephone. He returned shortly and announced that he just might have a solution to our tree troubles. Rather than explain, he directed me to get my car keys and follow him. We left the women to ponder the purpose of our trip and headed back down to the garage.

We took our car because the Hansens' vehicle still had the trees on the roof. When I asked Ben where we were going he directed me to his father-in-law's house about five blocks away. Lynn's dad Owen was well known for his wisdom and problem solving ability and I assumed that we were visiting him to seek his advice.

I was wrong. After a brief conference at the door Owen and Ben disappeared into the garage, emerging moments later dragging a huge coil of rope. I got the idea immediately. If we couldn't get our trees up on the inside, we would do it from the outside. I helped Ben load the rope into the trunk and we drove back to the apartment, planning this new offensive as we went. By the time we arrived back at 1005 we were as excited as a couple of little kids on Christmas Eve. The wives were a little dubious but agreed to go along with the plan.

We went back to playing cards to pass the time until we could put our plan into effect. Several hours and many glasses of eggnog later, shortly after midnight, we finally went into action. Carol went down to scout the lobby. She reported "all clear" via the intercom. Ben and I descended to the basement and brought up the trees. We laid them carefully in the snow right under our balconies. I looked up and spotted Lynn on her seventh floor balcony, waving encouragement at us over the edge of the railing. We left Carol to guard the trees and raced back up to our apartment.

We hauled the rope out on to the balcony of 1005, tied off one end to the railing and carefully lowered the free end over the edge. Coil by coil we lowered away, hoping we had enough to do the job. We did, barely. Carol tied the rope to one of the trees and signalled us to haul away. Now came the hard part. Ben and I were both young and fit, but trying to pull an inverted Christmas tree straight up in the air, from a perch ten stories above, was no easy task. Leaning out over the edge with our hips braced against the railing, we could use only our arms as we gathered in the rope, hand over hand. Foot by precious foot the first tree inched up the side of the building, past the second and then third floor balcony, brushing lightly against their wrought iron railing grilles as it went. The muscles in our shoulders and arms were on fire but we kept hauling, past the fourth and then fifth floors. Then at the sixth one of the large lower branches of our tree caught on the scrollwork of the railing of apartment 605 and our precious tree stuck fast. We were stymied. We tried to jerk it free but Lynn waved frantically from her balcony warning us of the noise and possible damage to the tree. We tried slacking off but to no avail. The tree remained caught. Now it was my turn to get innovative. I told Ben to tie off the rope and stay put while I went to the rescue. Grabbing my hockey stick out of the hall closet, I hustled down stairs to the Hansens' apartment and joined Lynn on the balcony.

With Lynn holding me by the belt at the back of my pants I leaned carefully out over the railing. From my precarious perch I used the hockey stick as a lever on the taut rope and tried to push the tree loose from its trap. It worked. The tree sprang free and swung out from the balcony. I turned the stick over to Lynn and directed her to use it to fend off the rope until we got the tree even with their balcony, then hurried back upstairs to 1005.

Ben and I took up the rope once more and pulled the tree one floor higher enabling Lynn to haul it in and onto their balcony. The Hansens had their tree. Now what about ours? Lynn untied the rope and dropped it back over the edge to the waiting Carol who secured the second tree. We hauled away again, but this time, having learned from experience, Lynn used the hockey stick right from the start, to fend off the rope and keep the tree from catching on any of the balconies. Puffing, panting and sweating, even in the sub-zero temperature, Ben and I strained to raise our tree to the tenth floor. By the time it passed the fifth we had our rhythm. Haul, hold, rest and haul; yard by yard the coils of rope accumulated on our balcony floor. Lynn's efforts with the hockey stick worked well and we cleared the sixth and seventh floor balconies without incident. Carol joined us on our balcony to lend moral support and encouragement. Then at the eighth floor disaster struck.

The tree was rising out of reach of Lynn's hockey stick. In a final attempt to keep it from being fouled on the balcony above Carol had pushed the tree away from the side of the building, at about the same time as we were hauling away. Our precious pine swung out all right, but then it swung back, just as we slackened off to restart. It struck the railing, tumbled over the edge and dropped onto the balcony of apartment 805. With a desperate tug of the rope, Ben and I tried to recover, but we were too late. This time the branches were trapped on the inside of the railing and the tree was stuck fast. Carol joined us on the balcony and the debate began.

We discussed several options, including using the rope to climb down the outside of the building to the eighth floor and free the tree. Fortunately sober second thought prevailed. In the end we were left with just one solution. We would have to wake up the tenants in 805 and solicit their help. The first problem was that we had no idea who lived there. However, the building did have an internal communication system. We checked the directory and found the tenant listed as B. Hard. The name meant nothing to Ben or me. But we got a break when the wives recognized the name as that of a woman they had made passing acquaintance with in the communal laundry room. Betty Hard was a widow in her late seventies. Her husband Bill had passed away that summer but she had stayed on in their apartment. The girls found her friendly enough, but she seemed sad and a little bitter at being left alone so late in life. This would be her first Christmas without her husband. How would she react to being roused from her sleep, in the dead of the night, by a couple of nuts who had managed to strand a Christmas tree on her balcony? There was only one way to find out. We decided to call first. Carol buzzed 805 on the intercom and we waited. No answer. She buzzed again and her effort was rewarded with a sleepy and faint, "Hello." We had made contact. Carol identified herself and fortunately Mrs. Hard remembered who she was. Carol launched into an explanation of our predicament. Mrs. Hard seemed confused and responded rather hesitantly to our request to visit. Then the intercom went silent.

We held our collective breath for what seemed like an hour; and then the intercom crackled back to life. "Well, there is a tree on my balcony all right," she said. "I guess you'd better come and fetch it."

Carol and I slipped quickly down the two flights of

stairs to 805. She tapped softly on the door and after a moment it opened to the length of the security chain and the heavily lined face of an older woman, framed in a mantle of silver grey hair, appeared in the gap. She smiled a hello at Carol and then her gaze rested on me, a rather large young man brandishing a hockey stick.

"It's okay," Carol reassured her. "He's my husband. May we come in?"

Mrs. Hard nodded. "Yes dear."

The door closed and we heard the sound of a chain rattling as she released the security lock. The door swung open and we entered.

The layout of the apartment was standard, the same as ours, but the furniture was from another era. The living room was neat and tidy, but as I made my way sheepishly across the rug to the door leading to the balcony I noted the signs of wear on the furniture and the patina of age on the tables. Carol paused to chat with and reassure our benefactor. I opened the balcony door and stepped out right into the middle of our tree. After tugging on the rope to attract Ben's attention I leaned carefully out and looked up to see his upper body draped over the railing, one arm waving enthusiastically in response. I freed the tree and hoisted it back over the balcony railing. Ben took up the slack and our precious pine swung freely once more, dangling 100 feet above the ground. Slipping back into the apartment, I mumbled a thank you to Mrs. Hard and left her talking with Carol while I hurried back upstairs to help Ben. Once again we hauled away and quickly completed our task, free of glitches.

Still puffing, but with smiles on our faces, we squeezed the tree into our apartment through the balcony door and set it in the waiting stand. Mission accomplished!

I helped Ben gather up the rope while Lynn prepared celebratory drinks. Despite the late hour, our exertions and the tension and suspense of our task had kept us wide awake. Carol returned from Mrs. Hard's apartment just in time to clink glasses and toast our success. She seemed, however, a little subdued. When I asked what was troubling her she told us.

"Did you notice that there were no Christmas decorations in Mrs. Hard's apartment?"

I hadn't, but Carol had and during their chat she found that the lonely widow seemed quite sad. Her husband had been her sole companion in life. They had been childless and his relatives and most of their friends now wintered in Florida. Mrs. Hard wasn't expecting any visitors for the holidays, so to her it seemed pointless to decorate. With only a week to go before the big day, our helpful neighbour was facing a bleak and lonely Christmas. It just didn't seem fair.

By now it was after three a.m., so we decided to postpone decorating our trees and get some sleep. The Hansens said goodnight and Carol and I got to bed.

Needless to say we slept in on Sunday, but after a late brunch Carol and I spent the afternoon decorating our tree. Although this was just our second tree we had lots of decorations. We had purchased several strings of lights and some ornaments and supplemented them with others donated by our families. We finished draping the last piece of tinsel, plugged in the lights and stood back to admire our handiwork.

The brightly coloured bulbs of the mini-lights we had chosen twinkled from their nests in the boughs, reflecting from the tinsel and enhancing the glow of the Christmas star that topped the tree. After supper we shared a quiet evening together, watching Christmas specials on T.V., wrapping gifts and putting the finishing touches on our preparations for Christmas day.

Lynn and Ben would be hosting their parents for Christmas dinner, but Carol's sister Gail and my brother Will both lived out of province and it was their turn to host the family dinner. Carol and I were quite looking forward to an intimate Christmas dinner for just the two of us in our apartment; we would do our Christmas travelling after Boxing Day.

It was back to work on Monday for all four of us, but the last few days before Christmas flew by and we soon found ourselves stuffing stockings and placing gifts under the tree. On Christmas Eve Carol and I gathered up some of those gifts and dropped in on the Hansens for a visit. Our main topic of conversation was of course our adventure with the trees. We recalled and relived the humour and tension of our escapade, gloating not a little over our success in outwitting the Watsons. When Mrs. Hard's name was mentioned Carol interjected,

"I saw her yesterday, in the laundry room. She asked about the tree and we had a laugh and a little chat. It's sad you know, her being alone at Christmas. We have each other and our families. She has no one. I feel sorry for her."

At about 10:00 Ben and Lynn saw us to the door; we exchanged hugs and wishes for a merry Christmas and Carol and I left.

As we stood in the hallway awaiting the elevator Carol seemed lost in thought and I noticed that she was still carrying one gift box. The elevator car arrived and we stepped in. I reached out to punch the button for the tenth floor but Carol stopped me and then pushed the button for the eighth. When I asked what she was doing she told me that we had one more stop and another present to deliver. We got off at the eighth floor and Carol led the way to the door of apartment 805. She knocked softly and shortly an eye appeared at the peephole.

"Yes, what is it?" asked Mrs. Hard in her soft voice.

"It's me Mrs. Hard," said Carol. "John is with me. May we come in for a moment?"

Her request was answered by the rattling of the night latch chain and then the door swung open.

"Merry Christmas!" we said in unison.

"Merry Christmas to you too," replied Mrs. Hard and she motioned at us to enter. The room looked the same as before. It was lit only by the glow of a single lamp on top of the television and there were still no decorations. I felt awkward but Carol seemed comfortable and got right to the point. She thanked Mrs. Hard again for helping us rescue our tree and then went on to gently chide her about not responding to her suggestion to put up some Christmas decorations.

I saw the look of sadness that stole across Mrs. Hard's face and settled in her soft blue eyes. I thought for a moment that she might cry, but she blinked back the tears and then smiled up at us.

"Christmas is for families and children, and young people like you, not old folks like me."

"Christmas is for everyone," said Carol, "including you! And here's a present to prove it." She placed the gift she had been carrying on the coffee table.

"Go ahead," she urged. "Open it."

"But I can't accept a . . ." started Mrs. Hard.

"Nonsense!" insisted Carol. "It's Christmas Eve!"

Mrs. Hard leaned forward in her chair, pulled the parcel to her, set it in her lap and began to unwrap. She worked slowly and deliberately. Her gnarled fingers grasped the stick-on bow and removed it. She set it carefully aside. The paper came off next revealing an unmarked cardboard box. Mrs. Hard folded open the flaps, removed the packing of crumpled newspapers and lifted the gift carefully from its nest. It was a ceramic Christmas tree, the one that Carol had made as a table decoration for our apartment.

"Oh, thank you," she said softly. "It's lovely, but I can't . . ."

"No buts," replied Carol. "You helped us with our tree; this one is for you. It's special, here look."

She took the tree from Mrs. Hard and placed it on the end table beside her. Carol plugged the electrical cord that ran from its base into the wall socket. The tree came to life. A frosting of hand-painted snow gleamed on the bows and tiny coloured lights twinkled brightly from the tip of each branch. Mrs. Hard reached out and lightly stroked the smooth ceramic surface with her fingers.

"It's beautiful," she said. "Thank you very much."

"You're welcome," said Carol. "And that's not all. John and I would like you to join us for Christmas dinner tomorrow."

"But I can't . . ." interrupted Mrs. Hard.

"I said no buts; it's Christmas," replied Carol. "You told me down in the laundry room that no one would be coming to visit you."

"Well, that's true," said Mrs. Hard. "No one is coming to visit, but I do have some family here. Quite close by as a matter of fact."

Not quite convinced, Carol challenged her claim. "Who?" she asked.

Mrs. Hard continued. " Well, you see my sister and her husband live right in this building. In fact, I think you know them: the Watsons? They are our building's superintendents. Now that my Bill is gone, I'll be eating with them this year. But thank you so much for the invitation anyway."

"The Watsons! They're your in-laws?" gasped Carol.

"Oh, oh!" I groaned, and glanced at Carol.

The expression of surprise and dismay on her face mirrored my thoughts. We sheepishly turned our attention back to Mrs. Hard. Embarrassed at being caught out we stood to leave, meekly ready to face the consequences of transgressing the "no live tree" rule. Thoughts of a New Year eviction crossed my mind.

Mrs. Hard was concentrating on her tree. Positioning it carefully, she adjusted it just so on the table. She gave a slight nod and murmur of approval, turned, looked up at us from her seat in the chair and then she smiled. The wrinkles of age faded from her face, replaced by dimples, and her bright blue eyes twinkled merrily as she grinned from ear to ear.

"Don't worry," she whispered, "your secret is safe with me! Would you like some tea and cookies?"

We spent the next hour, sitting in the glow of her tree lights, telling our new friend the whole story behind our adventure and Mrs. Hard shared with us some of her special memories of Christmases past.

Two Christmas trees: one forbidden, the other given. Two Christmas memories: one a first, the other perhaps a last. The spirit of the season is timeless and the magic of Christmas lives on.

Last Minute Tree

Christmas 1977 provided my wife Carol and me with one of our most cherished Yuletide memories.

We were expecting our first child and Carol was due to deliver in late November or early December. Keep in mind that Carol's name was a legacy of her December 25th birthday and being a Christmas baby she knew that things just might get a little hectic. So she worked diligently to complete the card writing, shopping, wrapping and house decoration prior to the blessed event. All that remained undone was the acquisition and set-up of our Christmas tree.

On December 10th our son Rob was born at Soldiers' Memorial Hospital. It was a long and difficult delivery, but both Carol and Rob were able to come home together a few days later.

As "rookie" parents we were on a steep learning curve and one of the things we were learning to cope with was sleep deprivation. Rob was a very good but a very hungry baby. Carol was breastfeeding and the frequency of feedings was well above the norm. This combined with all the other "new baby" chores resulted in Carol becoming very tired and things worsened when she developed a miserable cold. I tried to help out with changes, burping and laundry, but as an elementary school vice-principal with classroom teaching duties, it was also one of my busiest times of the year. By the time Christmas Eve arrived we were both exhausted and focussing on only two things: caring for Rob, and sleep. I came home from school that Friday night and found Carol sitting on the couch in the family room clutching a handful of tissue, alternating between wiping tears from her eyes and blowing her nose. I tried to console her but she pointed at the bare spot in the corner of the room and blubbered, "Tomorrow is Rob's first Christmas and my birthday and we don't even have a tree."

She was right. In all the hustle and bustle, I had forgotten to get a Christmas tree. We usually put up a real tree purchased from a local lot or cut at a tree farm during an outing with friends. But given the anticipated arrival of a baby, we had decided to pass on a real tree and go artificial for the first time.

Rob's cries signaled that he was awake and ready for his next meal. Carol headed upstairs to tend to him and I followed to say hello to my son. The two of them snuggled down to complete their mission together. Now I had a mission. I had to get a tree.

I checked my watch. It was almost 5:30 and in those days very few stores stayed open late on Christmas Eve to accommodate last minute shoppers. I had about half an hour to pick up a festive fir or we would be celebrating a treeless Christmas. I headed straight for Home Hardware.

I rushed into the store and spotted my quarry immediately. Perched on top of the display shelving near the checkout counters was a beautiful pseudo-spruce. Lighted and topped with a brilliant star, it was just the kind of tree I was seeking. I collared the first sales clerk I saw and explained my need. She escorted me down the aisle to get one but when we arrived at the appropriate section we discovered the shelf was empty. What was worse, not only did they not have any of that tree in stock, it appeared that they were completely sold out of all artificial trees.

The clerk offered to check the stockroom for me, but soon returned empty handed. Though sympathetic, there was nothing she could do. She apologized and left me standing forlornly in the aisle. Now what? It was too late to try another store, but I just couldn't go home treeless. Then the lights blinking on the display tree caught my eye. "Maybe, just maybe," I thought.

The staff was beginning to gather near the front of the store in anticipation of a prompt 6:00 p.m. closing. I again approached my sympathetic clerk and asked her if I could buy the display tree. She looked startled at first and then called for the store manager. I pleaded my case and explained my desperation. After all, the tree was no use to him after tonight, so why not sell it?

He smiled and agreed. He sent the woman off to get the box, called over a couple of stock clerks and directed them to begin undecorating the tree. He unplugged the string of lights and two staff lifted it down preparatory to dismantling it. "No!" I cried. "Stop! I'll take it as is!"

Our car at the time was a late 1960s land yacht of a Chevy, with a huge trunk. I was sure the tree would fit and there would be no need for assembly at home. I had acquired an instant Christmas tree.

Anxious to speed the process, the Manager complied, so I paid the bill and then drove my car up to the front door where the box was loaded into the back seat and the tree was placed carefully into the trunk. The lid wouldn't close tightly but a length of rope was produced to secure it. After a hearty exchange of Merry Christmases all around, we all set out for Christmas Eve with our families.

When I arrived the house was quiet. I tiptoed upstairs and, as expected, found both Carol and Rob sleeping. I unloaded the tree, carried it inside and set it in its appointed place. A couple of branches had fallen out of their slots and many others had been displaced, but after a few minutes of straightening a very natural looking spruce stood ready to be decorated.

The rest was easy. I re-strung the lights, hung our decorations and wound a silver tinsel garland around the tree. It was beautiful! Only one task remained undone, but I was saving it for later. I poured myself a drink and settled down to watch a little television.

As usual Rob woke early for his 2:00 a.m. feeding, promptly at 1:00 a.m. I got him from his crib and changed his diaper while Carol prepared to feed him. But that night, instead of taking Rob to her I invited Carol to follow us down to the family room. There she discovered a fully decorated Christmas tree.

"Merry Christmas and happy birthday," I said.

The smile on Carol's face was the best gift I received that Christmas. I seated her in the lounge chair right next to the tree, and delivered Rob into her arms.

There was one thing left to do. I picked up the last decoration and placed the Christmas star atop our son's first tree.

Glass Angels

Scuffing through the ankle-deep drifts of snow, I towed my toboggan along the sidewalk toward Mr. Novak's store. My six-year-old sister Cindy sat cross-legged on the seat pad, clutching the night's extra papers in her lap. With her face tilted to the sky she giggled and called out with joy, while trying to capture the fat flakes of falling snow on her tongue. It had been snowing for over an hour now and it looked like it would keep up. The snowflakes sifted softly down, drifting through the city lights, refracting their colours like so many prisms and freshening the streetscape with a clean coating of white. I liked new snow. Heralding the approach of Christmas, it seemed to muffle the harsh sounds of the city and temper the damp December chill, somehow making our whole neighbourhood seem warmer.

The street lamp at the corner of Shaw and Barton

was burned out, but the rectangle of light from Novak's store window spilled on to the sidewalk, marking our goal. We pulled up in front. Cindy clambered to her feet and ran to the door while I stood the toboggan on its end, banged it free of snow and leaned it against the wall. As usual Cindy was struggling with the heavy brass door latch, but when I added the pressure of my thumb to hers, it lifted and the door swung inward. The jangle of the small brass bells hanging above announced our entry and welcomed us to the warmth of the room. Mr. Novak looked up from the newspaper spread on the counter before him and raised a cautionary hand. But, despite his warning, the heavy plate glass window rattled ominously in its frame as the door banged shut behind us.

"Look Poppa Novak, it's snowing out!" piped Cindy.

"Ja, I see, and I'd like to keep it out," rumbled Anton Novak.

He pointed at our boots and in response we stamped them clean on the large rubber mat. The indulgent half smile on his lined face and the gleam in his sparkling grey blue eyes belied his gruff tone.

Mr. Novak treated his store like his home, which in fact it was. The lower floor consisted of three rooms. A large L-shaped section, which ran across the entire front of the building and down half of one side, served as the display area. A sales counter paralleled the foot of the "L" and ended just short of a curtained opening, which separated the store from the combined sitting/dining room, the kitchen, and the stairs leading to the rooms on the upper floor.

"Only four left tonight, Mr. Novak," I said, as I took the carrier's bag from Cindy.

Removing the newspapers I stacked them on top of the others in the *Telegram*'s wire display rack and hung the empty bag on the hook beside it.

"That's good for a Friday night," I added.

"Ja," he agreed. "Did you make your collections too Michael?"

"Yup, I got almost everyone."

I dug into my coat pocket for my ring of subscriber cards, unsnapped the leather collection pouch from my belt and handed them up to him. Mr. Novak studied the cards for a moment and then, flipping open the closure, he spilled the contents of the pouch onto the counter before him and started sorting. As he piled the bills and pushed the nickels, dimes and quarters into their places, I studied his gnarled hands. They didn't seem too bad today. They trembled only a little as he carried out his task, but a little was enough.

A young Mr. Novak had immigrated with his bride, Ada, from Eastern Europe, almost fifty years ago. A jeweller by trade, he spent almost a decade working for others, learning the language and the ways of business in his new land. Their dream was realized when they opened a small shop on Bloor Street, in west-end Toronto. It was a struggle at first, but skill, honesty and hard work were rewarded and the business prospered. Their son Peter was born and Novak's Jewellers became a fixture where, for the next thirty years, Anton Novak served the needs of his customers. Mr. Novak didn't just sell stuff; he was a craftsman. Everyone around the neighbourhood knew of his work and they came to him with their watches and clocks for repair and their precious stones to be set or reset, in custom designed rings and brooches. His skilled hands worked magic on all he touched, until his body betrayed him.

Advancing age and the onset of arthritis robbed Anton Novak of the nimble fingers, steady hands and sharp eyes needed for his craft; but he held on, delaying retirement in the hope that his son might follow in his footsteps. Peter had apprenticed with him and his work showed promise, but during the post-war economic boom the jewellery business began to change. Goods were more plentiful and ready-made items began to replace custom-made. Quantity, choice and price became the criteria for success and small stores like the Novaks' began to suffer. This, combined with the lure of the big upscale retailers, was too strong to resist and Peter chose a sales position with the prestigious Birks, in downtown Toronto, over a partnership with his father. A year later Mr. Novak downed his tools, held a sale and closed his doors for good.

I had known the Novaks for as many of my 12 years as I could remember. They were like grandparents to Cindy and me. Their jewellery store adjoined my parents' real estate office. In fact the two businesses shared the same building on Bloor Street. When Mum and Dad got divorced, he headed out west and she continued to operate Morgan Realty on her own. But caring for two small children made it difficult to be both owner and sales agent. That's where the Novaks came in. Whenever Mum was called out on business, Ada Novak stepped in as babysitter and kept an eye on us in their apartment above the stores. It soon became a permanent arrangement. As I got older, I spent more time with Mr. Novak downstairs in the workroom of the shop. I loved to watch and listen as he disassembled an item in need of repair.

Carefully laying out the parts on a red velvet cloth, talking all the while, he would tell the story of each watch or clock, its maker and its owner, as he traced the trouble and put things right. When finished, he would wind the timepiece and hold it to his ear. Nodding with satisfaction, he would pass the item to me for final approval. I would mimic him, nod solemnly in agreement and then, taking up my special cloth, put the finishing polish on before it was returned to the customer.

With the Novaks' help Mum found the time and energy to get Morgan Realty back on its feet, so when Mr. Novak was forced to retire and it came time for them to sell their shop, Mum listed it and did her best to find a new owner. There were no takers. Now after three years it was still sitting empty. But when the variety store beside our house at the corner of Barton and Shaw became available Mum didn't even put a sign on it. She sat down with the Novaks and the widow of the late owner; worked out a deal and Ada and Anton Novak began new careers.

Mr. Novak finished his sorting, put most of the money into the till and called me over.

"Here is your share," he said, as he handed over two dollar bills, seventy-five cents in quarters and my pouch.

"Thanks Mr. Novak." I put the money in the pouch, hung it back on my belt and turned to look for Cindy. I spotted most of her, sticking out of the curtain that separated the store from the family room.

"Cindy, stop that," I ordered.

Cindy pulled her head out from between the panels, made a face at me, looked over her shoulder at Mr. Novak and asked, "May I Poppa Novak?"

"I have been waiting for you," he replied and nodded. "Ja, go ahead."

Cindy squealed, clapped her hands together and darted between the centre fold.

"Come Michael," he said, motioning toward the curtain.

Mr. Novak shuffled along behind the counter and I walked to meet him at the doorway. We each pushed a panel to the side opening the way to the small sitting room beyond. The room was dark, lit only by the light filtering in from the store, but I could make out the shape of the Christmas tree in the corner. Cindy was seated on the floor beside it, an electrical cord clutched in her hand.

"Now, Poppa Novak?" she begged.

"Ja, it is time," he nodded.

Cindy pressed the plug into the socket and the tree came to life, flooding the room with brilliant light. I heard the sharp intake of her breath as she gasped in wonder; then she stood and began to study the ornaments suspended from the branches.

"It's so pretty, Poppa Novak," she whispered.

The Novaks had a very special Christmas tree. It not only celebrated the season; it told the story of their life together. A perfectly shaped spruce, it was wrapped in strands of fairy lights whose crystal clear bulbs nestled in the boughs, twinkling like a galaxy of tiny stars. Suspended from its branches were the angels. A host of delicate stained glass angels, each similar in size and shape, yet different in colour and design, graced the tree.

Individually hand-crafted by Mr. Novak, each angel was unique and had a meaning all its own. Together, they chronicled the family history. Their wings, robes and haloes covered every colour of the spectrum and when touched by the light from the bulbs they came to life, shrouding the tree in a rainbow of hues. No other decorations marred the beauty of the display.

Only one angel stood out from the rest: a magnificent golden angel, in honour at the top of the tree. Larger and more ornate than the rest, it presided over the assembly below. The lights enhanced its rich colour, reflecting its image on the ceiling where it hovered protectively over us all.

"Tell me an angel story Poppa Novak," begged Cindy. "Please, please!"

I held my breath, not knowing how Mr. Novak would react.

This Christmas, 1955, would have marked the fiftieth anniversary of Mr. Novak's life together with his beloved Ada. But last February age and a sudden illness had combined to take Ada's life, leaving Anton alone before that milestone could be reached.

Mr. Novak had grieved deeply but well and after a time he reopened the corner store. Peter moved back home to keep him company and things returned to normal. Oh, Poppa was a bit more gruff and grumbly with some of his customers and he kept a very close and critical eye on Cindy and me, much like Ada had, but all in all, he was the same Mr. Novak we had grown up with. However, Cindy's request would bring back cherished memories and I wasn't sure if Mr. Novak was ready yet to share them. I noted the play of emotion in his expression. First a wrinkled brow and set lips, then a brief sadness in his eyes as he sank deep in thought, and then finally, a smile.

"Ja, ja, all right little one," he said, "but first you sit here."

He took a seat and patted the arm of the big leather chair that sat in the corner across from the tree.

"Now, which of my angels tonight, should I tell the story of?"

Mr. Novak had told us the stories of his angels many times before, but we never tired of hearing them. Each angel had been made for a special reason, to mark an event in Novak history. I could recognize most of them now, like Peter's birth angel, the angel that marked their immigration to Canada and the ones that celebrated the opening of their store and their Canadian citizenship. I held my breath again, waiting for Cindy's reply, hoping that she would choose carefully.

"The golden angel, please, Poppa."

I saw the look of sorrow that flashed across Mr. Novak's face, but after a brief pause he began to speak, with only a slight catch in his voice revealing the emotion in his reply.

"That is my Ada's angel," he said. "It is the first angel I ever make and I make it for her. I learn how to make the angels when I was apprentice, in the old country. After my work with the watches and clocks, my teacher would show me how to work with coloured glass and lead, to make windows and designs. The angels were my favourite." He paused. "Ada and I were in love and we wanted to marry. My apprenticeship was soon to be over and it was time for me to ask her family for their blessing. The custom of our country was simple. I must give her an engagement gift, a special gift from the heart, a gift that I had made. This would show the family not only that I loved their daughter but also that I had the skill to support her. If her parents approved of my gift, a date for the wedding would be set. So fifty years ago I made the golden angel as my gift for Ada and placed it under her Christmas tree. When she opened it the beauty of the angel was matched only by the beauty of Ada's smile. The meaning was clear to all. We married soon after and came to Canada.

Each year since then I make more angels to tell the story of our life together and leave them under the Christmas tree for Ada to find, but this year . . ."

His voice began to quaver, but just then, thankfully, he was interrupted by the tinkling of the entry bells in the store. "Excuse," he said, getting up from the chair to serve his customers. Cindy plopped down in his place and sat gazing at the tree, but I followed Mr. Novak back through the curtain into the store.

"Good evening boys," said Mr. Novak, as he took his place behind the counter.

There were three of them, dressed in dark duffle coats. Their scarves were wrapped high around their necks, partially covering their faces and their toques were pulled down to eye level. They hadn't wiped their feet and they didn't acknowledge Mr. Novak's greeting. He tried again.

"What can I get for you?" he asked.

The shortest one stayed by the door and seemed to be studying the headlines on the newspaper. The one in the red toque ambled over to the bookrack and began to leaf through one of the magazines. The tall one approached the counter.

"Gimme a pack of Players," he muttered.

"Plain or with filter?"

"Ah . . . filter," the youth replied slowly. Mr. Novak took a pack of cigarettes from the display behind him, placed it on the counter and rang up the sale.

"That will be 48 cents."

"All clear!" said the boy at the door and suddenly, instead of money, a tire iron appeared in the hand of the boy at the counter.

The guy beside me grabbed the collar of my shirt and growled, "Don't move kid!"

"What do you want?" challenged Mr. Novak

"The cigarettes, and what's in the till," snarled the thief.

Mr. Novak shook his head slowly from side to side, hit the no sale button on the cash register and the till slid open. Removing the cash tray, he slid it across the counter toward the teenager. His buddy hustled me over to have a look. All that was there was my collection money and some change for the float.

"That's peanuts!" he scoffed.

"Where's the real money?" demanded the big guy, as he began tapping the shaft of the metal bar in the palm of his hand.

Mr. Novak just stood there with his arms folded across his chest, looking the creep right in the eye. I knew. Every afternoon around 5:30 Mr. Novak would tally the day's receipts and put them in the cash box for deposit. That box was sitting on the mantel in the other room.

"That's all there is. Take it and leave," growled Mr. Novak. Red toque pushed me toward Shorty and started filling his pockets, but the leader smashed the tire iron on the counter top and yelled, "Come on, Pops! Where is it? You better tell me or else!"

Cindy picked that moment to burst from between the curtains.

"Michael, Poppa, what's that yelling about . . .?"

For a frozen moment in time everyone stayed rooted to the spot, and then everything happened at once.

"Grab her Shorty!" yelled the big guy.

"No!" I countered and started struggling with him.

"I'll get her!" cried red toque, and he ran toward Cindy.

Cindy screamed and ducked back through the curtain, with the kid in hot pursuit. Mr. Novak and the leader raced each other down opposite sides of the counter toward the opening. Poppa beat him into the sitting room, but the big guy was close behind. I broke free from Shorty and ran after them, getting there in time to see red toque trying to pull Cindy from behind the big leather chair.

Mr. Novak roared, "Leave her!" Grabbing her attacker, he spun him around and pushed him right into his buddy.

"Get out of here," he ordered.

"All right, old man," said the big guy, "we will, as

soon as you show us what's in that tin."

He gestured with the tire iron and started toward the cash box on the mantel.

"Enough!" cried Mr. Novak.

Stepping into his path, he grabbed for the weapon and they began to struggle. Cindy was crying, I was yelling at them to stop and red toque was cheering on his leader. They broke apart. I saw the look of fear in the thief's eyes and then watched in horror as he raised the steel bar and swung. Mr. Novak tried to duck, but he was too slow and I heard the sickening crunch of metal on bone as the tire iron struck him high on the left side of his head. Stunned, he staggered backward, raising a hand to his temple. It came away bloodied. I saw the look of surprise on Poppa's face; then his eyes rolled back and he fell sideways into the Christmas tree, grasping at it for support as he slumped to the floor. The tree toppled and, as Poppa lay motionless on the carpet, it crashed down on top of him.

Cindy screamed, "Poppa! Poppa!" and I ran to help.

I knelt beside him and tried to lift the tree. There was a sharp crackling sound, some sparks, the lights flickered and then went out. Shorty appeared in the doorway, silhouetted by the light from the store.

"Somebody's coming!" he said urgently.

"This way!" said the red toque, as he pointed to the kitchen. "Out the back!"

"Go!" said the leader. Then he reached up and grabbed the cash box off the mantel and fled. I heard the jangle of the entry bells from the front of the store.

"Cindy, see who it is," I ordered. "Ask them for help!"

Cindy scampered past me while I searched Mr. Novak's pockets for his handkerchief. I found it and, folding it into a pad, pressed it to the wound to staunch the flow of blood.

"Michael, what happened?" demanded a familiar voice.

Mr. Novak's son Peter stood in the doorway, with Cindy clinging to the sleeve of his overcoat.

"They tried to rob the store, but your dad wouldn't let them and there was a fight and they hurt him and . . ." I babbled.

Peter joined me at his father's side and examined his wound.

"This is serious," he said. "Mike, go and call for an ambulance."

I ran back into the store, lifted the receiver off the wall phone behind the counter and dialled 0. After a couple of rings the operator answered. I asked her to send an ambulance and after a moment's hesitation and a few questions, she took the address and signed off. Just as I replaced the receiver the doorbells sounded again. I turned to look and sighed with relief when I saw my mother coming through the door.

"Mum," I cried, "come quick!" I pointed toward the sitting room.

"What is it Michael?" she asked, as she moved to follow.

"It's Poppa Novak; he's hurt. Hurry!" I explained.

We entered the sitting room together. It was still dark.

Mum reached over, flicked the wall switch and we had light. It was a grisly scene. Mr. Novak still lay on the floor, but his head was now cradled in Peter's lap. He was semi-conscious and groaning. Cindy sat in the big armchair, shoulders hunched and shaking as she cried softly into her hands. The tree had been pushed to one side, but multicoloured shards of broken glass littered the floor.

"Carol, thank God!" said Peter.

"What happened?" said Mum, as she moved toward Cindy.

"A hold-up," said Peter. "Punks! They roughed up Cindy and Mike and Dad is badly hurt! Did you get an ambulance Mike?" he continued.

The sound of an approaching siren made a reply unnecessary and I hurried back out to the front of the store to guide the ambulance crew. I returned with the attendants and they took over.

Peter rose and stood at the side and I went and stood with him, watching while they worked on his Dad. Mum comforted Cindy.

After a brief examination and a few questions about his health in general, they lifted Poppa Novak onto a stretcher and left for the hospital. Peter rode with them. The police arrived a few minutes later. The operator had called them too. Mum invited them into the kitchen, put on the coffee and directed me to get Cokes from the cooler for Cindy and me. We were nervous at first, but we knew one of them, Officer Lawrence, because he walked the beat in our neighbourhood. We spent the next hour telling what had happened, answering their questions and trying to describe the bad guys. By eight o'clock the police were finished and left to start their investigation. Shortly after that the telephone rang. It was Peter calling from Toronto Western Hospital, just a few blocks away.

The news was both good and bad.

Poppa had a severe concussion but thankfully not a fractured skull. He was going to be all right, but had been admitted and they were going keep him for a few days for observation. If all went well, he would be home by Christmas Eve. He was resting comfortably now.

Mum spent a few more minutes discussing security arrangements for the store and then hung up. It was time to go. Mum got the spare key out of the till. I hung the closed sign in the window and turned out the lights, she locked up and the three of us headed next door to our house. Cindy and I were sent straight off to bed. I don't know about her but I couldn't sleep.

I lay on my back in the dark, staring at the ceiling, reviewing the night's events in my mind. I was just drifting off when there was a knock at the side door. My room was right above the kitchen and the voices carried clearly through the air vent. It was Peter back from the hospital. Mum invited him in for coffee and they sat chatting at the kitchen table.

"Dad's feeling pretty rough, but the doctor says he's lucky. He got away with a concussion, some stitches and a giant headache," said Peter. "They're going to keep him overnight and run some tests tomorrow, but if everything checks out they'll let him out Sunday so he can be home for Christmas."

"That's great!" said Mum.

"Maybe," replied Peter. "Even if he's ready physically, I'm not sure about emotionally. This was the worst possible time for something like this to happen. You know, after I told him the kids were all right, the first thing he s asked about was the angels. In fact, when we got to Emergency he still had one of the wings from Mum's angel in his hand. He was more worried about it than he was about himself."

"How many were broken?" asked Mum.

"I don't know yet," Peter replied. "The big one for sure. I'll see about the rest when I clean up tomorrow."

"Mike and I can look after that. Aren't you working tomorrow?" said Mum.

"Well, that's the next piece of news." He paused. "I quit today."

"What!" interjected Mum.

Peter went on to explain. "You remember the idea I had for converting a section of Birks' downtown store to do custom work and in-house repairs? Myers the store manager really liked it and I thought things were set for next year. But his boss didn't; something about counter space and volume, so it's been dropped."

Mum interrupted, "But, what about . . .?"

"Carol look," he said, "five years behind a counter as a sales clerk is enough. You know my goal was to get off the floor and into design. I want to create, not just sell. It's clear now that's not going to happen with Birks, so I'm going to have to find another way."

There was silence for the moment and I heard the sound of cups rattling on saucers. Then Mum spoke. "So, it looks like it's been a banner day all round." I could hear the irony in her voice.

"I've got some news too. I gave Millie her notice today."

"Your office person?" queried Peter.

"Yes," replied Mum. "The neighbourhood real estate business is dying. It's all rentals and short term leases. All the action is in the suburbs. The big companies are taking over and I can't afford to compete or relocate."

They continued to talk, but I had heard enough.

"Holy mackerel, everything is messed up!" I thought. "Pete's job, Mum's business, Mr. Novak's angels." There wasn't much I could do about any of it . . . except, except maybe . . . the angels. That was it, maybe I could help with the angels! As I was mulling things over, my eyelids grew heavy and I drifted off to sleep.

Saturday morning dawned crisp and clear. Last night's snow had left me with work to do. After breakfast I got busy with my chores, shovelling our steps and sidewalk and the sidewalk in front of Mr. Novak's store. The closed sign was still in the window, so I went around back and knocked on the kitchen door. Peter answered and invited me in.

He had just made coffee and he used some of the leftover water to make a hot chocolate for me. We sat at the kitchen table. Peter had already called the hospital to check on Poppa and he brought me up to date.

"Dad had a good night," he said. "They're going to do some tests today, but he should be out tomorrow and home for Christmas Eve. He doesn't seem to care much though," he added.

"The angels?" I asked.

"That tree and those angels were his last link with the past, with Mum and their life together. Losing her was tough enough, but now even his memories have been taken from him."

I nodded in understanding and asked, "Have you cleaned up yet?"

"No, not yet."

"Well let's do that first," I suggested. "I can help and maybe things won't be as bad as they looked last night. Besides I've got an idea."

We went into the sitting room. Things were just as we'd left them. The tree was lying on its side in the corner and some of the angels were scattered on the rug near it. We tiptoed around the area collecting the fallen angels. Most were still attached to the tree. Thankfully these, and the ones on the rug, were unbroken. Peter placed them carefully on the mantelpiece. Unfortunately, some were broken. The top section of the tree had landed on the floor, beyond the edge of the carpet and pieces of golden glass littered the hardwood. Ada's angel had been completely shattered and three of the smaller angels were badly damaged. We did a quick count. Some were still missing.

Peter lifted the tree and I retrieved the lost angels from beneath it. The robe on one had a crack in it, but the rest were intact. They joined their mates on the mantel.

Peter stood the tree up and I crawled underneath to re-tighten the stand. After straightening the lights and replacing some broken bulbs, we rehung the undamaged angels. I plugged in the cord and the tree once again blazed with light. It was still beautiful, but it wasn't the same—not without Ada's golden angel.

"Well," I said, "it's not as bad as we thought."

"No," agreed Peter, "but losing the golden angel will break Dad's heart. But there's nothing we can do about that."

"Maybe there is," I said.

"Oh, I might be able to repair the damaged angels but there's no way to make a whole new angel," he countered.

"Could you do it if you had the pattern, some glass and stuff?" I asked.

"I think so," he said hesitantly, "but I don't know where . . ."

"I do!" I interrupted. "They're in Poppa's workshop. He let me help when he made last year's angel. I'm sure they're still there. I can get us in through Mum's office. What do you think?"

"Well, it's worth a try," he said. "Let's go have a look."

I unplugged the tree while Peter gathered up the damaged angels; we put on our coats and left together.

It was only a short walk. The building that housed Novak's old shop and Mum's real estate office was less than two blocks away, a few doors up the street from the corner of Bloor and Shaw. Bloor Street was thick with traffic and the streetcars were running linked to handle the holiday rush of commuters. Pedestrians crowded the sidewalk, hurrying to get their last minute Christmas shopping done.

I left Peter out front and went into Morgan Real Estate. Millie was in the office by herself. Mum must have been at home looking after Cindy. I gave Millie a quick hello, explained what I was up to and headed for the connecting door at the rear of the office. Slipping the bolt, I pulled the door open and stepped into Mr. Novak's abandoned workshop. I tried the light switch and was pleased to see the metal shaded bulb above the workbench begin to glow brightly. I made my way out through the curtain into the display area. The windows were papered over on the inside, but some of it had sagged away and I could see out onto Bloor Street. But I couldn't see Peter. I unfastened the lock and the heavy wood and glass door swung inward, hinges creaking.

Peter had crossed to the other side of the street and was standing, arms folded on his chest, scanning the storefront. He seemed deep in thought. I waved and called to him and he picked his way through the traffic, crossing the slushy street to join me in the doorway. I led the way back toward the workshop, but Peter took his time.

He surveyed the sales area, casting a critical eye on the empty wall racks and cabinets and pausing to stroke his finger through the thick layer of dust that coated the angled glass front of the old style display counter. Perhaps he was remembering the way things were, when watches shone and rings sparkled from their velvet beds in the gleaming wood and glass showcases.

"Hurry up Peter!" I said impatiently, breaking his train of thought.

"Sorry Mike," he replied. "All right, where is this stuff?"

We went back through the curtain and into the workshop.

I pointed to the shelves above the workbench and Peter began taking inventory. A selection of stained glass panes stood in a specially made rack. A scrap box of glass shards, in a rainbow of colours, sat beside it.

Peter talked out loud as he checked over the items.

We found glass cutting tools, files and small pliers for holding and bending the thin bars of lead that bordered and framed the stained glass shapes and there was a glass blower's torch for heating. But we could find no patterns to guide our work.

"Well, that looks like it. There's enough stuff here to fix the broken angels and even to make new ones, but it's not much use without the patterns. I wonder where Dad kept them?" mumbled Peter, as he rummaged under the bench.

I spotted a box on the top shelf. Clambering onto the bench, I stretched to reach it and handed it down to Peter. He blew the dust off and opened it. It was filled with patterns and templates of all different shapes and sizes. We had found what we were looking for! But, there was something else in the box.

Peter lifted out another glass angel. It was one I had never seen before. It was a small angel, like the others, but it was all one colour—a rich ruby red. And like some of the others the angel's robe was engraved with gold letters, but this one was unfinished. Peter held it up to the light and the angel glowed, highlighting the words NOVAK and SON JEWELLERS 19 __ . The date was incomplete. Peter held it for a moment longer and then placed it carefully on a shelf above the workbench, where it could oversee our labours.

"Well, what are you waiting for?" he said gruffly. "Let's get to work!"

We spent the rest of that afternoon repairing the angels. Peter sat perched on his Dad's swivel stool and I stood beside him acting as assistant, handing him tools and pieces of coloured glass. It was finicky work. Having the templates helped, but cutting the small replacement pieces for the damaged angels was tricky. Peter broke several wings before producing his first success. Once the glass was cut to size we had to cut and bend the thin lead bordering that held the broken pieces in place, remove and replace them, reshape the lead and then meld the ends together again.

But we got the hang of it, and began to make good progress.

As the afternoon wore on, we finished repairing all of the damaged pieces and started cutting glass for the golden angel. We both lost track of time, until I noticed Peter's watch. It was 4:30 p.m.!

"Holy mackerel; my papers!" I yelped. "I'm late. I've got to get going!"

"I'll finish up," Peter said. "Ask Millie to lock everything up when she goes. I'll let myself out. And hey, thanks for your help!"

"Ok!" I said. Crossing back through to the real estate office, I delivered my message to Millie and took off to get my papers. When I got to Novak's store the lights were on and Mum was behind the counter. I wasn't surprised. She had filled in before for Poppa Novak and I was pleased to see that Cindy had already opened my paper bundle and was stuffing the carrier's bag.

"You're late!" said Mum. "Where have you been?"

"Sorry," I replied, "I can't tell you yet. It's a surprise!"

"What surprise?" chirped Cindy. "Tell me! Tell me!"

"Later," I said. "Come on, let's go!"

I grabbed the bag and Cindy followed me outside. I loaded her and the papers on to the toboggan and away we went. I pulled and delivered while Cindy rolled the papers and we made good time, but it was well after six when we turned the corner back onto Bloor Street. Our route took us past Mum's real estate office and Novak's Jewellers. I peered through the gap in the paper, that covered the windows and I could see light seeping out from between the folds in the curtain at the rear of the shop. Peter must still be working. I thought about knocking but it was late and I was hungry, cold, and tired, so I knew Cindy would be too. Besides, I couldn't risk her finding out about the surprise and blabbing to Poppa Novak; we kept on until we reached the store.

Mum was waiting for us but she closed up immediately and we went next door for supper. While we ate we discussed our plans for Christmas Eve. Over the past few years we had established a holiday tradition of spending Christmas Eve with the Novaks. Peter would always visit and Mama Novak would heap the table with special foods from the old country.

Next would come the presents. The Novaks opened theirs on Christmas Eve. Cindy and I would eat quickly and then sit, squirming in our chairs, wishing dinner would end, because there were always gifts for us under their tree. After the presents were opened Poppa Novak would tell the angel stories. Oh, he always had to be coaxed, but once he gave in and began to speak, his words would weave a magic spell as the family history unfolded.

We knew things would not be the same this year, with Ada gone, but we hoped to keep up the tradition. Peter was to look after getting Mr. Novak home from the hospital. Mum would prepare the dinner. She had learned to make many of the traditional dishes from Mrs. Novak. Cindy and I were responsible for picking up the special items: the breads, cabbage rolls and cold meats from Kravchuk's Deli. We finished planning and Cindy and I spent the last hour before bed wrapping our presents for Peter and Poppa Novak.

Poppa's gift was a new sweater, a thick wool cardigan, dark green with soft suede patches on the elbows. It was perfect for him to wear in winter while tending the counter of his store. Cindy had chosen Peter's gift. She was always teasing him about his cold hands when he hugged her, so a pair of fleece lined leather gloves was wrapped for him. Mum let us stay up later than usual to finish and it was after ten before we got to bed. I was tired but it's hard to sleep on the night before Christmas Eve and I was still punching my pillow into comfortable positions when I heard Peter's knock at the back door. Mum poured coffee and I listened in as Peter brought her up to date.

The tests had gone well and his father would be released as scheduled, late tomorrow. He went on to tell Mum about the angels and my chest swelled with pride when Peter described my part in their repair. The coffee cups continued to clink on their saucers and Mum started to share our plans for Christmas Eve. But I had heard enough and drifted off to sleep, satisfied that Poppa would be home for Christmas and the angels would be there to greet him.

December 24th dawned sunny but cold. In 1955, Sunday in Toronto was a family day. The churches were full, particularly at this time of year, and even though we attended the early service we had lots of company. All but the neighbourhood stores were closed and there were no newspapers, so even Cindy and I had a day off. Late in the afternoon a taxi delivered Peter and Poppa to the front door of the variety store and we were all there to meet them. Peter helped his father out of the back of the cab, but Poppa shook off his steadying hand and shuffled slowly toward the door. His head was bare, but partially wrapped with strips of gauze bandage holding a pad in place over his wound. Stiff shocks of gunmetal grey hair stuck out at random angles from between some of the folds. His eyes were dull with pain or sadness and I could tell from the slump of his shoulders that although his wound had been treated, his heart was still broken.

Cindy ran to hug him. He smiled, knelt to embrace her, and for a brief moment the sparkle returned to his eyes; but it was gone when he rose and took her hand to follow me. I led the way into the store, through the curtain and into the sitting and dining room. Mr. Novak carefully avoided looking into the tree corner.

Mum had already lighted the candles on the table and places were set for the five of us. The food sat piled on the sideboard and delicious aromas were seeping from the covered dishes. When he saw the display Poppa straightened a little, stood taller and questioned Mum.

"This is your work?" he asked.

Mum nodded and Poppa Novak moved closer, took her hands in his and said solemnly, "I thank you. Ada would be pleased." I saw the tears welling in Mum's eyes, but she fought them back with a smile and then directed us to sit.

Anton Novak took his customary place at the head of the table. Cindy and I sat on one side, with Mum and Peter seated side by side across from us. Ada's chair sat empty. Poppa bowed his head and led us in the grace.

Peter poured wine, even for me, and we began to pass the serving dishes around the table. As we heaped our plates with food the conversation was formal and stilted. Pass this, pass that, please and thank you. Everyone was polite. Too polite. We talked about the food, the weather, Poppa's recovery, and the food again. Mr. Novak said very little. He sat quietly and when he spoke I could hear in the tone of his voice the sadness in his heart. Every once in a while I would catch him staring at the empty chair and the unlit Christmas tree, hidden in the shadows beyond.

The conversation died off, replaced by the rattle and clink of cutlery on plates. Cindy squirmed in her chair, unable to hold her excitement in.

"Poppa Novak, may I?" she piped, and pointed to the tree.

"Ja, go ahead little one," he said, but his voice lacked its usual enthusiasm.

Cindy slipped out of her chair and scampered toward the tree. Taking the cord in her hand she pressed it firmly into the socket.

The tree came to life and the sitting room filled with light as hundreds of tiny stars blazed on the boughs. Every colour of the rainbow was splashed on the walls of that room and the golden angel, in all her glory, once again spread her wings over the assembly below. Peter had done his work well.

Poppa's shoulders squared and he sat taller in his chair. The lines faded from his face, the years melted away, and his grey blue eyes sparkled with emotion.

"But how . . ." he started to say.

It was my turn. "Peter did it!"

And I went on to tell the story of our search for the patterns and the rebuilding of the angels.

Poppa smiled and nodded as we told our tale and favoured me with a gruff "Good, very good, Michael," when Peter related my contribution to the project.

We ate while we talked and happiness returned to the room. Mr. Novak motioned toward a crystal decanter on the sideboard and Peter passed it to him. Poppa poured, filling first Mum's glass, then Peter's and then his own. He paused and then poured a little of the amber liquid in my glass. Cindy looked at him expectantly but he shook his head.

"No, not yet little one. For you the water."

Anton Novak stood, raised his glass and motioned for us to do the same. He looked at each of us in turn and spoke softly, in his gravelly voice.

"Thank you, to all of you. You have made an old man young again. Come, join with me in a toast. A welcome to the angels!" And we drank.

Even though I barely sipped the fiery liquid seared my throat, bringing tears to my eyes. Cindy giggled and pointed at me, but Poppa frowned at her and then smiling at my distress said "Ja, is good, Michael?" before banging his empty glass down on the table and announcing, "And now, the presents!"

We left the table and gathered near the Christmas

tree. Cindy sat right beside it, Mother and Peter took the love seat opposite and Poppa settled into the big leather armchair. I acted as Santa but Poppa directed my activities. He would point to a particular parcel, I would check the tag and then deliver it to its owner. There was something for everyone.

First a silver necklace with a tiny birthstone for Cindy, next Mum showed off a gold bracelet and Peter slipped a signet ring on his finger, all from Mr. Novak. And he personally strapped a new watch on to my wrist. There was still more.

I began to deliver our presents. Peter's gloves fitted perfectly and Mr. Novak replaced his worn sweater with his new cardigan. The pile of presents dwindled until only two were left. Peter pointed to the smallest and I checked the tag. It read simply, "Dad." I delivered it to Poppa Novak. He removed the wrapping, split the tape seal on the box with his nail and unfolded the covering of tissue.

He paused momentarily, staring down into the package, and then lifted his gift from the box. It was the ruby angel; the one I had found. Anton Novak raised it carefully to the light and the golden letters gleamed NOVAK and SON JEWELLERS 1956. The inscription had been finished. Peter reached out to steady his father's trembling hand.

I saw the look that passed between them and then together they hung the newest angel on the tree.

A single present remained. I checked the tag and placed it at Mum's feet. She rechecked the tag and then turned toward Peter.

"You shouldn't have," she said.

Peter just shrugged off her comment and motioned

toward the gift.

Cindy chimed in, "Open it Mummy; open it!"

Following her instructions Mum untied the ribbon and carefully removed the outer wrapping. It was a shoebox. Setting it on her lap, she lifted the lid.

There, nestled in a bed of soft green tissue, lay a golden twin to Ada's angel.

"Oh Mummy, she's beautiful," whispered Cindy. "Is she for our tree?"

The room was silent as Mum stared down at the symbol of Peter's love and commitment. Then she turned to face him and raised her eyes to meet his gaze. Peter nodded slightly. Mum responded with a shy smile and accepted his proposal with a soft but firm, "Yes."

I wasn't quite sure what to do and when I looked to Poppa for help he just shook his head slowly from side to side and placed a finger to his smiling lips. Cindy broke the spell.

"Tell us an angel story Poppa Novak, please, please," she begged, and Poppa replied "Ja, ja, all right little one," and he patted the arm of the big leather chair, "but first you sit here."

Cindy snuggled into the space beside him, laid her head on his shoulder and waited for her cue.

"Now which of my angels tonight should I tell the story of?" asked Poppa.

Cindy pointed.

"Ah, that is the angel that I make when . . ."

And that Christmas Eve, and many more, would be filled with memories and promise, and the magic of glass angels.

About the Author

John Forrest, of Orillia, retired after 35 years as an educator (teacher, Principal, and Director of Education) and began writing about the exceptional events and wonderful people that have enriched his life. Drawing on his experiences he strives to recreate the emotion and impact of those special moments in life that touch us all. His short stories have been published in the nostalgia magazines *Reminisce* and *Good Old Days*, the news magazine *Capper's*, in the anthologies *A Cup of Comfort for Inspiration* and *Chicken Soup for the Christmas Soul* and as the lead story in the syndicated feature page *The Front Porch* which appears in over 100 newspapers in the American mid-west. His works have aired on CBC Radio's *First Person Singular*, and *Richardson's Roundup*, and have won first place in competitions held by *The Toronto Sun*, *The Orillia Packet and Times*, and *The Owen Sound Sun Times*.